CHAINSAW SISTERS

JACOB FLOYD

Nightmare Press
Louisville, KY

Nightmare Press is the horror imprint of Frightening Floyds Publishing

Cover Art by Lydia Burris
Graphic Design by Holly Wholahan

Thank you for reading! If you like the book, please leave a review on Amazon and Goodreads. Even if you don't like it, please still leave a review.

To keep up with more Nightmare Press news, join the Anubis Press Dynasty on Facebook.

Other works by Jacob Floyd:

The Pleasure Hunt
Night of the Possums

Paranormal nonfiction with Jenny Floyd:

Louisville's Strange and Unusual Haunts
Kentucky's Haunted Mansions
Haunts of Hollywood Stars and Starlets
Indiana's Strange and Unusual Haunts

TABLE OF CONTENTS

Introduction: Chainsaws and Other Crazy Things

Chainsaw Sisters...........................01

OTHER TALES:

Street Cheese………………………………………..68
Monsters of Wooded Hollow…………………………..81
Undead from Outer Space…………………………...88

About the Author

Other Releases from Nightmare Press

INTRODUCTION: CHAINSAWS AND OTHER CRAZY THINGS

The blueprint for *Chainsaw Sisters* came to me after an indie press I was involved with put out a submission call for stories inspired by the trash horror films of the 80s. Initially, I was going to call it "She Talks to Chainsaws" because I get many ideas for stories and titles from songs I like. This one came from the Black Crows song, "She Talks to Angels". After about five minutes of careful consideration, I determined that title totally sucked and that it would be desecrating a fantastic song, so I decided to call it something else. *Chainsaw Chatter* was my next pick. I wasn't entirely happy with it, but I thought it would make a passable working title until I fleshed out the details and came up with something better.

So, as Jenny and I sat around, with her listening to my idea as I tried to figure out the purpose, conflict, and direction of the story, we decided on a name. Since the protagonist was going to believe her sister was talking to her through her chainsaw, we decided "Chainsaw Sisters" would be appropriate. This helped me create the main character because it reminded me of an old pro-wrestling tag team from the original G.L.O.W. – the Heavy Metal Sisters, Spike and Chainsaw. In the end, there would be no similarities between them and the main character, but it did provide a little inspiration.

That left the task of coming up with the main character's name—which, for a large part of the book, the main character is the chainsaw. I wanted her last name to be Chainsaw. But what first name would go good with that? Well, since the story was to be reminiscent of 80s slasher films, we decided it would require a very 1980s female name. For me, that was easy – Amy, it doesn't get too much more 80s than that. And it had a ring to it, so Amy Chainsaw was officially born.

As with any of my stories, the influences are obvious, at least to me, and probably to those who are fans of the films, songs, books, and/or shows that inspire me. And I'm never afraid to own up to them. Naturally, the story drew heavy influence from *The Texas Chainsaw Massacre*, which is one of my all-time favorite film franchises, the original being, in my opinion, one of the best movies ever made. I think the landscape for the bulk of the book has that desolate wasteland atmosphere that prevailed in *Texas Chainsaw*. It is a setting I have often found to be beautifully lonesome but deadly and nightmarish all the same.

But that wasn't the only influence. The other main character—the flesh and blood human; the one that's not a deadly weapon—was highly inspired by Cecile de France's character, Marie, from the 2003 French horror film, *High Tension,* known in its home country as *Haute Tension*. Those of you in the United Kingdom would know it as *Switchblade Romance*. I pictured Sis looking a lot like her—strong, frightening, and blood-splattered. A very similar surreal psychological imbalance exists in the book that did in that movie.

Those two films pretty much inspired the flesh-splattering mayhem coating the pages ahead. In retrospect, I think *Kill Bill* has something to do with my inspiration, too. I don't know how much, but Tarantino's genius has influenced me for about twenty years or more. But, as for the non-gory aspects, the underlying story is a little bit of crime, mystery, and science fiction. I cannot pinpoint a particular inspiration in those genres for the story, but it no doubt comes from the numerous crime and mystery films I always loved, as well as the many sci-fi and horror anthology series I used to watch on TV.

Anyhow, once I had the story figured out, I jotted down a few notes and let it lay while I was finishing up *Night of the Possums*. Not longer after, I parted ways with the publisher I was going to submit this to due to personal differences. But another publisher that I'd always liked opened up submissions for an anthology they were going to release, and so I wrote *Chainsaw Sisters* and submitted it. A few months later, my story was shortlisted and under serious consideration. But for personal reasons, the publisher postponed the anthology. A few weeks before I received the email informing me of this, Jenny and I had actually discussed the possibility of me expanding *Chainsaw Sisters* and publishing it ourselves. I had already decided to follow the short with another story, so it made sense.

In the publisher's email, they had stated that they would understand if I withdrew the submission and so I did. But not with any ill-will. I informed them that I completely understood their situation and I withdrew the story, letting them know my intentions.

With all the other projects we had going on, the story got pushed aside for a while. I did outline it, adding quite a bit more details and turns, but never finished the outline. Crunch time came a few months later and I just sat down and wrote it, going through the short, adding and subtracting, dividing (no multiplying), and making it fuller. The tale took over and grew organically, developing into a mystery on top of the bloodbath it already was. What resulted was, in my opinion, a pretty layered and genre-crossing story.

Chainsaw Sisters was a new adventure for me. I've already done gore. But I challenged myself to write a quicker and more dialogue-driven story without as much introspection and scene description. My first two novels don't have a ton of external dialogue. Most of the talking is in the characters' heads. That still a big part of *Chainsaw Sisters,* but I created more conversations for this one. The other two novels are also full of scenic details, and I was a lot more to the point here. *Chainsaw Sisters* is also non-linear, which is another new approach for me. With everything I write, my goal is to grow as a writer, and I really think I did with this one.

Now when it came down to it, the story was still too short. I wanted to put a little more into the book before I released it and I was in luck. I had spent most of the first part of 2018 writing short stories for anthologies—something else that was new to me because I'd never been a short story writer. In 2018, I wrote a few short stories. Among them were "Chainsaw Sisters", "Street Cheese", "Undead from Outer Space", and "Monsters of Wooded Hollow".

Influenced by the film *Street Trash*, I wrote "Street Cheese" for a pizza horror anthology and it was rejected. I was later invited to write a short for an anthology compiled and published by a fellow author, and the theme was to be sci-fi and zombies, which were both out of my writing wheelhouse, so I was glad to take it. That resulted in "Undead from Outer Space". "Monsters of Wooded Hollow" is something I wrote for my blog, *Jacob Floyd's Ghosts and Monsters*, and then decided to unpublish it from that platform and maybe put it in a collection.

I had been a bit bummed about the time I spent writing those shorts most of the year. I felt I could have been working on my monster horror novel for which I still haven't completed the outline but have wanted to write for about two years now. But, once I realized *Chainsaw Sisters* was going to be shorter than I wanted, I realized that was the perfect opportunity to make use of those shorts. Jenny said it best. She said, "See, it all came together. You wrote those short stories last year and now you get to publish them yourself."

So, I hope you enjoy *Chainsaw Sisters*. It was a lot of fun to write, and a very rewarding challenge. It's not for the squeamish, as it gets gruesome in parts. I also hope you enjoy the shorts that follow. It's a diverse little collection of tales from my weird and warped mind.

Thank you for reading,
Jacob Floyd

CHAINSAW SISTERS

CHAPTER ONE: AMY CALLING

I stood outside of my father's house staring at the tumbledown shed in the backyard. It hadn't been used since his rheumatoid arthritis got bad a few years ago and was now in sad condition. The grass out back was slightly high and there was some junk and garbage strewn about. If I remembered the inside correctly, it was rather cluttered and dirty.

I first heard Amy calling to me from somewhere inside that shed. I don't remember how I got there, or what I was doing before I heard her. It was as if I woke up from the darkness of a dreamless sleep and found myself rooted to the spot, staring at the shed, confused as to how Amy could be yelling for me from inside.

Even Amy was a hazy memory. There wasn't very much about her that I could remember. I wasn't even sure how I recognized her voice. She was hard to hear at first, like the scratchy, fading voice at the end of a dying phone, but it soon became so clear that it sounded like her voice was in my head. Something about it was familiar and I could swear it was hers. I couldn't remember her face at all, but something kept telling me it was Amy.

You see, Amy disappeared years ago. I don't remember how or when, or what life was like before she had. Everything was hard for me to recall. But, I knew she was gone and I hadn't seen her in a very long time.

So why did I hear her voice calling to me from the shed?

Sis, I'm in here. Help me.

"Amy?" I called and started across the backyard, nearly tripping over a rusted gas can from God knew what era.

As I waded through the grass, I don't know which was racing faster—my mind or my heart. Confusion, excitement, and sorrow mixed to create a bittersweet stew of insanity, like strawberry pie stuffed with a ruptured stomach. Questions cut through my mind like the teeth of a serrated knife.

How is Amy calling to me?
When did I get here?
Where was I before?
What's my name?

Wait…Amy only called me "Sis." What's my name? Dear God…I can't even recall that! What in the hell has happened to me? I know this is my father's land, but what's my father's name?

I just call him Dad.

Maybe Amy will have the answers.

I pushed aside the wobbly wooden door, trying not to cut myself on the broken, jagged bits of wood peeling off like tree bark. It barely slid open against the grass, scraping and chugging through nature's thick tendrils.

The air inside was thick with the dust rolling off the scattered debris, and musty from years of weather and rot. If Amy was in here, I couldn't imagine her breathing long enough to live. I almost choked before cupping my hands around my nose.

"You in here, Amy?"

Over here.

Her voice was listless and distant. I glanced in the direction of the words and saw only a large table in the corner. The wood on the wall was rotting away and the bright afternoon sunlight pounded its way into the murky interior. A few items lay on the table, but I didn't bother to strain hard enough to see them.

"I don't see you? Where are you?"

I'm dead. That's why you can't see me.

Shivers of a cold reality rippled through me, freezing me in the shed's oppressive air.

"What do you mean you're dead? I can hear you."

This is not me. Only my subconscious speaking to you. What's left of me now calls to you.

"How?"

Through a conduit.

"What do you mean?"

Look in the corner. I am on the table.

I stepped deeper into the shadow of odoriferous shed, drawing nearer to the table. There were a few tools lying about, and pieces of chopped blocks and rusted chains. Various pipes lay both cut and complete, gathering rust, dust, and spider webs. But Amy did not speak to me through these items, for there was something else, something far more distinct, on the table. It did not take long for my eyes to find her vessel.

Now you see me, she said.

Bathed in the small ray of sunlight shining on the table was a heavy-duty woodcutting chainsaw with a twenty-inch blade. The item was out of place, as if it was brand new and had never been used. I picked up the heavy tool and looked for a brand name, but there was none. There was no writing anywhere on it. I set it back down on the table, intimidated a little by its power.

Yes, Sis. You have found me.

"I don't understand, Amy. Why is your spirit inside a chainsaw?"

Because Sis, I need you to avenge me.

"What happened to you?"

As I told you, I am dead. I did not simply disappear.

"How?"

Several men kidnapped me and killed me.

I couldn't believe it. I felt like one of those meatheads in a carnival that took a cannonball to the gut. I hadn't deluded myself too long after her disappearance. For a while, I'd hoped she'd just gone off somewhere and not told anyone—maybe started her life over. From the little bit I could remember about our dad, it wasn't like living to work for him was an ideal station in the world, especially for someone with any ambition.

What was Amy like? Was she content to work hard and go on with life? Or had she wanted to do things, like travel, create, be spontaneous and not know where the next day would take her? I actually pictured her running off to the mountains somewhere, or crossing the western deserts, maybe heading into California to be an actress, or a porn star, or a vagabond.

But, I didn't know. I remembered almost nothing about her. I barely even remembered myself. I think I liked the small towns, and manual labor. I had the muscles to show for it. I thought I didn't want to be at my dad's forever, but I could have done hard work somewhere else, like a blast furnace or steel mine. At least I think that's how I was.

To be honest, I don't remember much about Amy's disappearance. I just know that one day she was there and then she wasn't. I don't think I ever considered her being murdered. Maybe the thought was somewhere in the dark part of my mind, but I didn't acknowledge it. Maybe I was blocking it out, as they say, and that's why my memory was so goddamn foggy. Tragic reality might have finally set in. Thinking someone you loved had met such a fate was something no sane person wanted to envision.

Am I sane, though? Standing in here talking to a chainsaw I think holds the spirit of a sister I can barely remember says otherwise. But, life isn't always what it seems. I believe in other realms—ghosts and UFOs and beings from other dimensions—so, I'm willing to accept Amy's spirit may have chosen a station to store her dwindling life energy in, and managed to manifest the strength to seek me out and speak to me. A chainsaw has some form of life, right? The electricity that courses through it. It's not like a desk or something that just sits there and needs no power.

"What did they do to you, Amy?"

Horrible things, Sis. I don't want to tell you. It would hurt you too much.

The chainsaw began to ripple and fade into a watery blur. The tears were hot in my eyes. I felt my strong arms wobbling beneath me as I leaned against that nasty old table.

"Do you know who they are?"

Yes.

I grabbed the handle of the chainsaw and dragged it to me. I looked down at the teeth, the sharp, wood-ripping blade, and the chain that could tear trees to pieces. I began to feel a surging need to kill flow through me. This time, when I lifted it up, it didn't feel as heavy. It was as if fate had deemed that I was to wield this mighty device for another purpose. The chainsaw was my Excalibur.

"Then tell me," I said to the blade.

CHAPTER TWO: FIRST KILL

Under Amy's direction, I left my dad's house with the chainsaw over my shoulder, letting it dangle down my back. The blade did not cut me; it didn't even touch me. My bicep met my forearm and the hardness of my taut muscles felt empowering. I was strong and the weapon that hung behind me was even stronger. Together we would realize Amy's revenge.

I pulled the chainsaw back and held it before me.

"You really are Amy, aren't you?"

I am.

"I haven't gone insane, have I?"

No.

I smiled and let Amy dangle beside me.

She then continued to guide me.

The house is at the end of the street. The man that lives there set me up. He helped the killers kidnap me. He orchestrated it. Make him pay for that, Sis.

"Oh, I will, Amy. I will."

Can you do it? Can you kill him?

"I think so. I certainly feel like I can."

At this moment, you're angry about what he did to me. But when you finally look him in the eyes, will you be able to tear into his flesh and carve out his insides?

"That's very graphic, Amy."

Soon, you will face with that graphic reality. Can you hack it?

I smirked. "Nice choice of words."

Can you?

My smile faded. "We will see."

When I had left Dad's, I was all balls-to-the-wall, ready to splatter this man's body all over his kitchen. But now that I grew nearer to his home, doubt *was* beginning to creep in. Amy sensed it. She was right. Words and thoughts are not three-dimensional. They are not reality. They are nothing without substance, without action. All that mattered were the events on life's timeline. If I came face-to-face with this son of a bitch and couldn't saw him to bits, then I might find myself suffering Amy's fate.

I think you can do it, Sis. When you look into his eyes, you will see him for the wretched beast he is. You will know that he is a low-life animal that deserves to be treated like cattle. You will feel the urge to maim him, slaughter him, and turn him into nothing more than crimson jelly twitching on the floor.

Her words filled me with desire—a craving to kill. I felt the liberating bloodlust surging through my body. For a second, I remembered something from my past: swinging on a swing set when I was a child, looking into the face of a very angry man. Who he was, I don't know. The memory hung on for a second and then went away, and I wanted to kill.

I came to the last house on the right. Ahead of me stood a small, grungy shack with white vinyl siding heavily stained from years of neglect. There were three windows in the front, one of them badly cracked, two of them missing screens, and all of them grimy. The top screen of the storm door hung loose from the top right corner, flapping in the soft afternoon breeze. The grass was at least two feet high.

I reached the driveway and asked, "Is this the house, Amy?"

Yes. Go to the back door and let yourself in. He never locks that door.

I looked up and down the street to see if anyone was watching. It looked empty out here. The only sign of life I saw was a black car coming down the street. I stopped for a minute to let it pass, trying to look inconspicuous despite the massive chainsaw slung over my shoulder.

The car slowed as it got near me. The window was rolled partially down. I saw a pair of eyes and a black baseball cap watching me. The driver stared at me as he drove by. I thought he was going to say something. When he and I made eye contact, it made me a little nervous. It was as if he knew me, or was watching me.

"Who is that, Amy?"

I don't know.

"He looked like he knew me."

Probably wondering what you plan to do with me.

"Should we go through with this? He seemed to have gotten a pretty good look at me."

I wouldn't worry about it.

"Okay." I trusted her and continued on my way.

The few houses on this street were so far apart that it was unlikely anyone could see me. They were all just as shitty as this one. I doubted anyone would even care to remember me if they saw me. I couldn't recall if I knew anyone around here, but I didn't care. The man inside had to die, so I could not balk.

I walked up the oil-stained driveway; small tufts of grass lined the numerous cracks in the concrete. There was a beat-up Chevy car parked near the house. I made my way around back and saw a rusty blue truck parked in the high weeds near a small garage. There was noise coming from inside the structure and I paused.

"Is that him, Amy?"

No Sis. That's a friend of his. He comes over sometimes and works in the garage. He's an evil man. Make sure you kill him, too.

"Did he hurt you?"

Oh yes. He did.

"What did he do?"

Don't worry about that. Just get the guy inside first. Then come back out for the man in the garage.

"What if he hears me and calls the cops, or leaves?"

He won't hear you. If he does, he certainly won't call the police. He won't run, either. He's one of those rowdy cowboys always looking for a fight. He'll probably come right for you. If he does, you'll be ready—won't you?

"Yes."

The backyard was vast, like a giant lake of grass, and the garage was way in the back, dozens of yards away. Amy was right—he probably wouldn't hear me killing the man inside. I was surprised I could hear *him* in the garage.

Much of the paint on the backdoor was peeled off. There was only a solitary step on the porch and I climbed it and grabbed the knob, which was unlocked as Amy said it would be, and let myself in. The kitchen was a mess, but not filthy. It looked like housekeeping took place maybe twice a week. The place didn't really stink; it just smelled like a house: a little musty with the stench of humanity, the lingering aroma of a meal cooked hours ago, and a hint of garbage that needed to be taken out. I'd expected complete filth.

A television was on in the front room, so I stepped cautiously in there. There was a couch, a recliner, and a TV with a lamp next to it. I saw the back of a man's brown, shaggy head raised above the chair.

That's him, Sis. Kill him!

I gripped Amy's handle tighter, ready to lift her and destroy the man on the couch. But something stopped me. As I looked at the back of his head, my own head began to swim. My eyes went hazy, my vision fading to black, and white, and I blacked out.

I felt cold and distant, far removed from that evil man's living room. My mind experienced a strange metamorphosis that I couldn't even begin to explain. An overpowering ringing pervaded my ears, seeming to swallow them whole. The shrill was so torturous I wanted to scream but couldn't.

What was this?

Monsters.

I felt monsters around me.

I went to lift Amy but she wasn't there.

Panic set in.

I could not fight the screaming darkness alone.

Sis?

Amy?

It's okay. I'm still here.

Where are we? I can't see! I can't hear!

We are together. That's where.

I don't understand.

You will.

The ringing became so powerful it sounded like people talking. My head was ready to split. The voices chattering felt like needles in my brain.

Make it stop, Amy!

The ringing soon faded and I heard whispering voices in the darkness around me.

Wake up, Sis.

I did – and that's when the visions began.

FLASHBACK I

I sat with my gloved hands on the steering wheel, staring out at a darkened parking garage. This place was unfamiliar to me, but the fear I felt was not from the strange surroundings, but from the sense that something terrible was about to happen. More than a sense, it was knowledge. I knew something bad was going to happen because I had been here before despite recognizing nothing about it. This was not a dream, but a memory. A memory coming from somewhere so far removed from my brain that it was foreign.

I looked around for anything that might tell me where I was and what was going on. There was nothing but parked cars and dim bulbs to keep me company. Across the lot, I saw a closed metal door with a sign that I couldn't read it. I was alone with no idea where I was. The clock on the dashboard read 2:47. Judging by the stillness around me, I assumed that it was in the AM. All I could do was wait.

In a few seconds, the clicking of heels on concrete let me know that my window was down about halfway. I looked in the direction of the sound and saw a woman with curly blonde hair walking purposely across the lot. I looked around to see where she might be going and could only guess which of the few cars she could be getting into. Beyond one of those cars, I saw a masculine silhouette step from behind a van and approach the woman, who kept looking at the ground. She didn't see him until it was too late.

By the time the woman looked up, the man's fist was about to crack her in the face. I jumped at the sound of flesh and bone colliding. The woman, much smaller than her attacker, stumbled back a few steps and hit the ground, dropping her purse. The man stepped quickly up to her and hit her again, knocking her onto her back. The smack carried on the still air and the dread I had felt began to give way to anger, and when the man grabbed a handful of the woman's hair and started pulling her up, I couldn't stop myself from starting the car and driving over to them.

I moved as if I was in a dream. I couldn't tell if I was in control of this or not. The man quickly yanked the woman off the ground as I drove forward. I watched in helpless rage as he dragged her to a black van, opened the doors, and tossed her in. He then crawled into the van with her and dropped a few more punches. At that point, I wanted to ram the car into him. Had it not been for the possibility of hitting the woman too, I would have done it.

I brought the car to a soft and quiet halt about ten feet from the van. I left the door open when I got out and walked over to it. The man was too involved in what he was doing to see me. When I stopped a few feet from him, he had his back turned, and I considered attacking him. Just as I made my move, something told me to stop, so I did. I looked hard at him. He wasn't too old, probably late thirties, early forties at the oldest, and he was overweight.

The woman's legs dangled out from the back of the van. She didn't move. He must have knocked her out. I hoped the piece of garbage hadn't killed her. There was a needle in his right hand and I watched in horror as he injected it into his victim's arm. She groaned and moved her head side to side before going completely limp.

What had I just witnessed? Why was I standing there doing nothing? I should be stopping this.

My mind now screamed for me to move, but it was a scream from the beyond. It was too far away for me to obey. My muscles burned to make a move for the man but my body remained still. I didn't know what to do. I felt like I had two minds working against each other.

The man threw the needle into the vain and rolled the woman all the way inside. When he turned back, he saw me and jumped. Almost instantly, his faced twisted in rage and he thrust a stubby finger towards my face.

"What the hell are you doing? Get your ass back in the goddamn car!"

I obeyed without hesitation and waited for him to pull out. Once the van passed me, I quickly fell in behind and followed the man towards the parking garage exit. As I drove along behind him, I could swear that I knew exactly who that woman was, only I was unable to access that memory.

Just as we came to the exit, the whole world went black once again.

FACE TO FACE WITH THE NEEDLE MAN

Sis, open your eyes.

Amy was speaking, this time she was close. I opened my eyes and saw the back of the man's head once again. The parking garage had vanished and the living room had taken its place. The Needle man was still in his raggedy recliner watching TV.

Who was that woman? Was it Amy?

No, it was not me.

Then who was it?

Another victim in a crowd of victims. Another reason to kill. You said you could kill when the time came. The time has come.

Amy was right. I could not let her down, so I did not hesitate. I told Amy I would avenge her, and I meant to. With the choke and the chain break activated, I pressed the decompression valve and set the chainsaw on the floor, stepped on the rear handle, grabbed the front handle in my left hand, and pulled the chain with my right. The engine roared to life like a predator ready to strike; the man in the chair jumped from his seat. When he turned around, his wide eyes saw the screaming blade. He held out his arms and tried to speak, but could not be heard over Amy's war cry.

I charged past the chair and went for him with the blade out. The chainsaw felt natural in my hands, as if it was a necessary part of me. He dodged aside, climbed on the couch along the window, and tried to scramble away. He was yelling something but I didn't hear him, and didn't care to. He fell off the couch and hit the floor, but sprung back up just before Amy could slice off his leg. After retreating into the kitchen, he tried to throw a chair, but the seat hit the underside of the table when he lifted it, knocking the chair from his grasp. When he knelt to grab it again, the tip of Amy's blade nicked the top of his head and he fell backwards to the floor, screaming with his hands on his scalp.

There was only a small amount of blood, but the sight of it made me want more. He lay on his back, using his feet to scoot back towards the cabinets. There was no room for him to escape. His ugly face and saggy eyes looked up at me, full of fear. I had no sympathy for him.

And that's why I drove the chainsaw into his left leg.

The skin broke, the blood exploded, and the bone cracked. I didn't cut all the way through, but it was enough to make him scream. I didn't fuck around after that, either. After he sat up to grab his leg, I drove the chainsaw upward like a golf club and sawed right through his face, starting under the chin, all the way up through the skull, splitting his head in half. What a glorious mess that made. His white cabinets and refrigerator looked like the abstract art of an asylum inmate. He collapsed to the floor in a bloody clump of dead weight.

I eased off Amy and her roar became a soft whir, like the satisfied purr of a cat. Amy was like a lion with mighty teeth stained from the kill. The first kill was a success.

"I did it, Amy."

Yes, you did. You did well, and you did the right thing.

"Did I, Amy? Did I do the right thing?"

You saw what he did to that woman.

"Was that vision real?"

It was. And she was not the first, nor was she the last. There have been many.

"Why did I see that? Was that memory mine?"

After a few seconds of silence, my heavy breathing the only sound in the room, Amy spoke.

Yes…and no.

"What the hell does that mean?"

Another brief silence from Amy.

You'll know in time. Right now, you still have a job to do.

"Oh yes," I said and turned my face toward the small kitchen window to my left.

I could see the garage in the distance. The truck was still there.

"My work is not yet done here."

12

CHAPTER THREE: SECOND KILL

I kicked open the back door, knocking it partially off its hinges, and stood on the porch looking out across the backyard. When my gaze fell upon the truck, I began to feel sick again. My stomach churned and twisted. I was able to zero in so closely on the junky vehicle it was like looking through binoculars. I could see every detail: all the dings and dents, the flecked paint, the rusted spots, the fading blue stripes running along the side. I could even see where the tread on the tires was wearing down. I saw it so well I thought I could touch it.

All interest in the truck was lost when I saw the man emerge from the shadow of the garage. He was tall with shaggy hair and dirty blue jeans. Automotive work had stained his hands black. Sweat glistened in the hair on his chest, dark specks of dirt and oil splattered on his bare skin. A wave of revulsion almost knocked me over. I knew him. Not by name but by sight. I'd definitely seen him somewhere before. But where?

He reached into the bed of his truck and then the horror hit me in the gut. I felt my knees buckle but I don't know if I fell because I was cast back into the dark.

FLASHBACK II

This memory was hazier.

I opened my eyes to find myself seated at a table littered with beer cans, cigarettes, and overflowing ashtrays. Several other men sat around it. The scumbag I had just killed, Needle man, sat to the right of Garage man, who was taking hits from a water bong passed to him from a younger guy sitting to his left. The younger man had two other young fellas at his left and another sitting behind him. The four youngsters looked like high school dropouts on TV shows.

The bong bubbled for a bit and Garage man held in the smoke before letting it out slowly and passing the bong back to the youngster, who then laughed like an idiot. Garage man turned to Needle man and began talking as if in the middle of a conversation I had missed.

"Like I was sayin', the driver was sixteen and the other was probably younger."

"Where did you say they were from?" asked Needle man.

"The girl drivin' had a license from Utah. The other didn't have no ID. I bet she's real young. I think she'll work quite nicely." Garage man smiled and I felt an impulse to jump over the table and bash his head in with one of the glass ashtrays.

I may not have remembered much about myself, but deep down I felt like I wasn't a violent person at heart. This sudden propensity to maim people seemed to come from some place hidden, some place far away, unfamiliar and altogether new. It scared me, but it was also exhilarating. Years of rage seemed to have been building in me and I had yet to realize it, and now it was rising towards the tip, ready to explode.

"Where are they now?" asked Needle man.

"I got 'em tied up and pumped full of junk out in the shed. Been injectin' 'em fer a couple of days now. Won't be long 'fore they're so hooked they'll suck and fuck anything for a fix."

The repulsive Garage man let out a greasy chuckle and lit a cigarette. I thought Needle man was bad—which he was—but this walking mass of anal crust was far worse. He was the scum of the Earth and I wanted to cry thinking that Amy had fallen into his vile hands.

"Sawyer will sure be happy when he hears that," Needle man said.

"Damn straight he will be. I always bring him the good shit." Garage man wiggled about in his chair for a minute and said, "You know, I'm feelin' a little in the mood, myself. I could go sample them girls in my shed again, but they're all dirty and stinkin' up the place, and I don't feel like washing 'em."

He turned in his chair and yelled, "Patty! Git yer ass in here!"

A woman from another room called back, "What?"

Garage man became angry and said, "I said git yer ass in here, you deaf bitch!"

A sickly-looking junkie came into the room. Her sleeveless shirt was dirty and her bony arms were covered with track marks. It must have been another one of his hookers. Imagining the atrocities he visited upon her made me almost vomit. I didn't know the grip addiction could have on a person, but it must have been powerful if any woman would be willing to fuck this revolting cave troll to appease it.

"And I said what do you want," she replied.

Garage man stood up, adjusting his belt and pulling his pants up repeatedly. "I'm feelin' frisky. Git in the bed," he motioned with his head towards a pulled-out futon behind them.

The woman rolled her eyes. "No."

She started to turn away but he grabbed her stick of an arm and yanked her back. "What the fuck did you just say to me, whore?"

"I said no, motherfucker. Get the hell off of me." She tried to pull away but Garage man just yanked her arm down hard; the joint popped with a loud snap, causing her to squeak and double over. Her eyes squinted shut and her mouth opened in pain.

"Bitch! Don't you fucking tell me no!" he yelled.

She tried to pull away but he was too strong and her arm hurt too much.

"Git in the bed!" he leaned over and screamed into her ear.

"Fuck you, you whoreson!" she cried.

Garage man's face twisted with rage, and he let go of Patty's arm to grab a handful of her hair instead. He then pulled her up and slapped her so hard across the face that she fell back onto the bed.

He stood over her and said, "Don't you call me no whore's son, you slut. I ain't gonna let you talk 'bout my mama like that. She ain't no whore like you."

Patty laughed, spitting up a little blood. "That's not what it means, you stupid sack of shit."

Garage man leaned in again and backhanded Patty with a resounding smack that snapped her face to the side. "You sure are getting' mouthy, girl. I think I might hafta stuff that mouth with something to shut you up."

After making that half-witted statement, he looked back at those of us around the table with a satisfied grin, as if to say 'Y'all hear that? That was funny'. Everyone but me laughed. You could tell he really considered his threat clever.

Patty, however, shot it down by saying, "What you got ain't big enough to fill nobody's mouth, you teeny-weeny prick."

Garage man raised his arm to punch and threw himself down upon her, slugging her three times as hard as he could. The sound of his fists crashing against her body nearly made me leap from my chair to throttle him. But something held me back, just like before, and it frustrated me nearly to tears.

There's nothing you can do, Amy said. *This has already happened. You cannot change it.*

Then why torture me by making me watch?

Because you must know what kind of people these men are.

The young boys looked on in perverted fascination, chuckling at the brutality. Needle man just kept drinking his beer as if he had seen this so many times that he was impervious to its immorality.

After Garage man finished his barbaric assault, he said, "You gonna do what I say and open up now?"

Patty turned her head and said, "Fuck you."

Garage men then grinned and said, "Now that's 'xactly what I mean."

He then grabbed the waistband of her yoga pants and began pulling them down. They ripped in the middle as she thrashed against his violation. Eventually, he tore the pants completely off, hit her hard enough to knock her silly, and said, "If y'aint gonna do it willingly, I'll just make ya."

One of the young punks laughed and another one said, "Awesome." I wanted to kill them all.

My vision then went hazy again. I did not blackout completely. It was more like the onset of a severe head-rush. Everything twinkled into black and red before returning slowly in a shower of yellow sparks. Once I could see clearly, I was looking at Needle man and Garage man standing at the back of the van from my first vision. We were gathered outside a house somewhere at night. Garage man was crawling into the van with the unconscious woman. Her legs were hanging out the back of the van again.

"Don't think you junked her up enough, Earl," Garage man said.

Needle man then answered, "Guess not. She was squirmin' and this idiot was walking up to the van when I was trying to get it done." Earl pointed at me.

Garage man looked at me and asked, "Why the hell were you doin' that?"

Before I, or whoever I was, answered, the woman groaned and began to move her legs. It caught Garage man's attention and he quickly lost interest in my answer.

"Goddamnit!" he said and moved further into the van.

"Be careful, Joe," Earl said. "Can't rough her up too much just yet."

"Don't worry," Joe said. "I'm just gonna have a little fun."

Joe straddled the woman and started hitting her. The impact made her legs jump and move. Hot rage boiled through me. I wished I'd had Amy in my hands so I could slowly cut this fucker apart and make *his* legs jump.

After he finished beating her, he started taking off her clothes. Earl said, "We ain't got time for this, Joe."

"Aw hell, it won't be but just a second."

As Joe took down his trousers, I was overcome with so much fear, sorrow, and hatred that I lost my breath. My vision became shaky and chaotic, like I was riding on an earthquake, before going black again. I was thankful for this because I couldn't bear to see any more.

When the blindness left me, I opened my eyes to a new horror. I was looking up at a moldy ceiling with a dim bare bulb shining off to the left above me. I felt a ripping agony all through my body and found myself screaming in a deep, unfamiliar voice. The worst of this terrible pain was coming from my feet, so I looked down at them to see what was causing it.

That's when I saw Joe again. He was standing at the foot of the table with a blowtorch in his hand, and the flame turned onto my feet. I could feel the flesh melting and it was the worst pain I ever felt. I tried to sit up and kick out at him, but I was strapped down. The restraints were loose enough for me to move, but not enough to allow escape.

As I watched the flame burn my flesh, I got a better look at my feet and realized something equally unsettling. They were broader than my own and the toes were much longer. I then began to take notice of the rest of my body. I lay shirtless on the table, looking at a torso that was clearly not mine. The chest was flat and the stomach hairy, which did not match my description by a long shot. I also had on men's underwear and could see a large bulge sticking up from the crotch.

What am I seeing here, Amy?

She did not answer.

Joe turned the blowtorch off and looked at me. "Had enough yet?"

Whoever I was, they did not answer.

Joe walked over to the side of the table and stared down at me. "You know what you did was pretty fuckin' dumb, right? You thought you could just walk right in here and do whatever you wanted. I tried to tell Sawyer you was a bitch, but he wouldn't listen. Sometimes he can have a soft spot. But not me. I got no sympathy for motherfuckers like you. In fact, I take a lot of joy in hurtin' ya."

Joe reached into the pocket of his jeans, pulled out a pocketknife, and flipped it open. "You done saw too much, and I ain't gonna let ya' see no more. Not that it matters much because y'aint got much time left no how. But this here will be fun fer me, nonetheless."

Joe then lowered the tip of the knife slowly towards my left eye. My body struggled beneath the restraints that held me but it was no use. I saw a blur of silver just before the knife plunged into my eye, killing it and sending waves of pain rippling through my body. My other eye went blind as I faded out once again.

JOE'S GARAGE

I barely remember storming to the garage. But when I came back to the present day, I was already across the lawn and heading into the darkness. The volume on the radio was at full blast. I recognized the song...it was saying, "Just dance" and that's what I had come to do – a twisted tango of flesh and steel grinding together, with the roar of the chainsaw and the wails of the man rising into the afternoon sky.

I stepped inside, feeling no fear of the beast that waited to greet me. He had many random car parts on the ground next to a stool, tools scattered all around them. There was an engine hoist in the center of the spacious garage. The man was looking at me as soon as I came in. He looked even meaner in person. His face was hard and his eyes were hateful, his arms tight and slightly bulging. He was a strong man, that much was clear. But I am a strong woman and I had murder in my heart.

As I walked in, I looked at the ground to make sure I didn't trip on anything. How intimidating would that have been if I Dick-Van-Dyked my way through the garage, slipping and tripping on everything in sight? That wouldn't have done me any good in the psychological warfare department. I noticed Amy was dripping blood onto the floor, and had left a spotted trail of red liquid behind me. Maybe that would win me some psyche-out points.

Joe looked at me curiously for a second. His face did not convey his thoughts. He was as stony as the floor.

"I know what you did," I said.

Joe smiled and said, "Do ya?"

I did not reply. I simply stared at him, imagining his insides exploding all over the floor.

He pointed at Amy and said, "That Earl's blood?"

"Earl's the guy in the house, right?"

"Yep."

"Then it's Earl's blood."

"You know I'm gonna kill you, right?" he said.

The sound of me revving Amy up was my response. Joe smiled again and picked a 60-inch Wedge Point Crowbar up off the floor. I ran at him with Amy in front of me, ready to drive her hungry teeth deep into his body. But Joe was as quick as he was strong. He swung the crowbar and landed a heavy blow on Amy's blade, knocking her from my hands.

She hit the floor and slid away from us. I lost my footing and stumbled right into Joe. The impact of our bodies hitting caused him to drop the crowbar. He took a few steps back as I regained my balance. While Joe was teetering sideways I shoved him, but without much force; I wasn't in a good position when I struck out. He only fell back a couple of feet before getting control of himself.

When he righted himself, I didn't give him a chance to get set. I charged at him and swung, landing a heavy right across his jaw. He fell back but threw a lightning-fast punch that cracked me right in the forehead, shoving my head back and dropping me to one knee.

This was the opening Joe needed. He came at me, arms outstretched, and grabbed me around the throat and started strangling me. I quickly grabbed his wrists and planted my feet under me, bringing my body to a crouched position, and then pushed up with all my strength. My legs were powerful and I managed to force Joe back a bit but could not stand up all the way. He maintained his chokehold but it was slipping. I managed to rise and take some steps forward with my knees still slightly bent. Joe resisted me and I ended up pushing his arms to the side. We started to spin around, locked in that position before I was able to pull his fingers off my neck.

After I broke his hold, he kicked at my stomach and only managed to hit my side, which still hurt. His boots were steel-toed and I felt like a car hit me. I bent over and he grabbed me by my hair, which was short and hard to hold onto. But he still yanked my head around a little anyway.

I pulled away as hard as I could, some of my hair coming out. When I stood back up, he was already coming towards me. I threw a haymaker against the side of his head and rocked him; he threw one back and knocked me against the wall. He was on me in a flash, pushing his knee into my gut. I tried to punch him but we were too close and he was already throwing me to the floor by my neck. As I went sideways, his foot shot out and knocked my legs out from under me, causing me to fall. In a desperate attempt to stay standing, I reached for him, grabbing his waistline and practically ripping the fly open before I hit the floor.

I rolled onto my back and looked up at him. He looked down at his open pants and smiled. "You musta read my mind. Glad to know you want it as much as I do, 'cause you was a-getting' it anyway."

"You ain't man enough to handle me, bitch-boy."

He then threw himself upon me, hitting me two times in the face. I brought a hard shot into his stomach, which was incredibly solid, and it did nothing but earn me two more punches that had me seeing stars. I then lay there dazed, thinking about how I had failed Amy.

My arms fell limp and Joe slapped me one more time for good measure. He then spit blood on me and said, "You sure are a tough bitch. I'm gonna show you what I do to tough bitches."

Get it together, Sis, or you're going to be next.

Amy's voice was frantic. Something vile was about to happen to me if I didn't move. I shook my head to wipe away the cobwebs and saw Joe had leaned back and begun pulling his pants down the rest of the way.

"I already know what you do, you sick bastard," was all I could think to say.

He smiled and started slipping his pants off.

20

This is your chance, Sis. Move now!

Going only on the instinct to survive, I moved my legs and struck out, kicking Joe right in the side of the head. He fell onto his back and I quickly got up and yanked his pants off. He had no underwear on and was fully nude. His legs fell open after I pulled the jeans off his ankles. I threw down the jeans and grabbed his left ankle, lifted my left leg and brought my foot down as hard as I could right into his testicles. He cried out immediately and I gave them another kick. I then grabbed his other ankle, held his legs open and dropped my right knee onto the soft spot in between, bringing all my weight down with it. The blow was spot on. His balls were smashed beneath me. He squealed and gagged, rolling from side to side with his hands cupping his junk.

I leaned forward and punched him in the side of the head, knocking the other side hard against the floor. His cranium made a beautiful thud against the hard concrete. I brought my left around and hooked him in the middle of the face, causing blood to explode from his nose upon impact. Even though this rattled him good, I clasped my hands together and brought them hammering down into the side of his face for good measure. He was dazed after that.

I stood back up with a plan, and I needed some strong rope to make it happen. I looked around the garage and found some Japanese bondage rope and nearly got sick imagining the twisted purposes it had most likely served. He had quite a bit of it, so I tied two ropes to each of his ankles and then used another to bind his wrists. Once he was good and secure, I rolled him onto his front and dragged him across the garage to the engine hoist.

The hoist was a telescoping gantry crane with an I-beam running across the top. I cranked it down low enough to tie the ropes on Joe's ankles to the beam, leaving his legs spread about four feet apart. I then raised the crane to around nine feet, leaving Joe hanging upside down. I retrieved Amy from the floor. Now Joe was the one spread open and helpless, right where he belonged.

I stood behind him, listening to his whimpers. Amy must've frightened him because he grunted and groaned and begged for mercy.

"What's wrong, you piece of garbage? You don't like the feeling of being vulnerable?"

"Please, let me go. Don't do this."

I smiled. "Look at you shrivel up. You're not so bad now, are you?"

"Please," he repeated.

Show him no mercy, Sis. He's a monster.

"I won't, Amy."

"What?" Joe said frantically.

"Shut up, trash!" I yelled.

"What do ya want from me? I'll give ya anything I got."

"Give me? Maybe I'd rather just take what I want, like you do."

Joe's eyes seemed to shine with realization, which soon subsided to fear.

"Okay, okay, I know what I did was wrong. But, I got problems, man. You know? I need help. How about you let me down and we can do something about this. I'll turn myself in."

See, Sis? By his own admission. I told you he's a monster.

"I never doubted you, Amy."

The man looked confused. "Who the hell is Amy?"

I raised my sister and said, "Like you don't know, dumbass."

The fear on Joe's face changed quickly into rage as he yelled, "You dumb fucking bitch! Let me go or I'll fucking kill you!"

I laughed in his face and said, "Oh, you're a real tough bitch, aren't you? Let me show you what I do to tough bitches like you." I yanked Amy on and she began to roar again.

"Why don't you say hello to Amy one more time, motherfucker?"

I lowered the blade towards his pelvis. He began to thrash in anticipation of the oncoming pain.

"Yeah? What do you think about that, whore? You stupid slut!" I yelled, calling him the names he loved to call his victims.

When Amy's blade came down into the crack of his ass, he howled like a mad werewolf. Bile and blood shot out as I pushed the blade in further, grinding his cock and balls into torn, pulpy flesh. He screamed and shuddered on the beam, rocking the entire crane. But I didn't stop. I drove Amy deeper, cutting through the groin and into his guts. Blood splattered and flowed all over the garage floor.

"How does that feel?" I screamed, feeling the veins in my neck bulge. "You like that? Doesn't feel good, does it?"

I laughed as I continued to dig in. The deep rut I tore into his body made his legs spread further apart. Amy kept going down into him. I felt the blade strike his spine. The sound of the saw intensified as it chipped away the bone. Small white shavings shot out, one cutting hard across my cheek, drawing blood. Intestines dripped from his stomach, bits of them sailing through the air as Amy shredded the bastard's insides. Bodily juices bathed the area, some of it slightly burning my skin. I assumed this was stomach acid as a large chunk of something fleshy flew out when Amy passed through his abdomen.

As Amy chewed her way into his chest, I knew I'd reached a point where I could go no further. Even though she eviscerated his ribs and lungs, and broke away his breastplate, she had become too heavy for me to control. I could do no more.

Pull me up, Sis, before I get stuck.

I turned Amy off. Bending my legs and pulling with all my might, I withdrew her from Joe's obliterated body. Once again, I likened her to Excalibur and fancied myself Arthur pulling her from the stone. But there was not the ringing sound of steel gliding on rock that sang through the air; it was the wet, squishy noise of hateful metal ripping its way through a man's conquered body.

After releasing Amy, I stepped around the dangling meat-sack to take a satisfied look at our work. The body was nearly torn asunder. Unrecognizable innards hung loose from the giant cavities dug along his corpse. Blood cascaded like a waterfall to the floor, coating his face and filling his gaping mouth, frozen in an agonized wail. His wide eyes were stained red. I lifted my sister up and gazed at her. She was bathed in the beautiful destruction we had orchestrated together.

"How did we do, Amy?" I asked.

Wonderfully—I can feel the surge of his death in my blade. It's like feasting after being famished.

"I know. I feel it, too. It's like rebirth. Ending these lives begins a new life. It just feels right."

Amy was silent for a second, perhaps savoring the victory.

Good. You understand.

"I do. Words can't describe it, but I understand."

I knew you would.

I looked around the gore-stained garage for a second, drinking in the justice.

"Lead me to our next victim, Amy."
With pleasure, Sis.

CHAPTER FOUR: A QUARTET OF KILLS

After reducing Joe to a drained sack of mangled meat (which was better than he deserved, in my opinion), I mostly hoped we were done. Though I couldn't recall much from my life, I was pretty sure going on a killing spree was a new adventure for me. I tell you what, though - it was a lot of work. My legs were aching something fierce and Amy was getting heavy in my arms. I noticed a burning sensation at the base of my skull. When I reached back to feel what was causing it, I felt a line of small bumps where the irritation was. I must have suffered an injury at some point.

What in the hell had happened to me?

Though I wanted to call it quits, I would be lying if I said there wasn't a part of me that wanted more. When I felt Amy grinding into that bastard's body, cracking his spine and blending his viscera like a zombie protein shake, it felt good – like, awesome good. I wanted to keep going, chopping that slimeball into so many pieces that no one could have recognized him as a human carcass. That would have been fitting because he was barely human anyway. And it wasn't just the fact that he was a reprehensible beast that made me love slaughtering him so much, and it wasn't even the fact that he had planned to violate me—yes, those were unquestionably contributing factors—but I just simply enjoyed it. Killing him made me feel alive. Torturing him satisfied some sick hunger to inflict suffering on someone. That rather scared me and I tried to ignore that desire.

So when Amy told me we weren't done, deep down I was excited.

"So who do we kill next?" I asked almost eagerly.

No ring of scum can operate without its band of witless thugs to do its dirty work.

I looked down at Amy and said, "Go on."

The pieces of shit who carry out the crimes for these bastards are four local degenerate boys in their late teens and early twenties. The leader's name is Brock. His right-hand man is Tex. The other two are Bubba and Bobby Jack. Just like their names imply, they are a bunch of dumb country fucks. These pathetic perverts do the shit the other cowards don't want to bother with: robbery, assault, break-ins, all that kind of stuff. They are mean kids, but they are also kind of chickenshit when someone stands up to them, so that might give you an edge. But be careful. They're not above ganging up on someone and two of them carry guns – Tex, the bald guy with thick eyebrows, and the tall skinny punk with shaggy brown hair – that's Brock. If you can take them out first, then do it. The other two only carry knives.

"Okay, where are they?"

Every evening they park on the corner of Burns and Danziger to smoke pot and get drunk while waiting for Earl to come and give them their marching orders. Well, it looks as though Earl won't be joining them this evening. Since these dimwits have no real direction in life, they'll probably sit there all night. By the time you get to them, they'll be so drunk and stoned they won't know what's going on.

"What if someone else comes by?"

That is not likely. Neither of these roads has been used much since they cleared out all the houses. The city up north decided to build a small airport here a few years ago but the project fell through. Now it's just a desolate stretch of land with woods and open fields. That's why these idiots use it. But if someone does happen to come, just run into the woods unless I say otherwise.

I nodded, too lost in thought to speak. This was dangerous. When the exhilarating frenzy that came from the kill wore off, the heavy reality of the situation set in. I was playing for keeps in an unwinnable game. I had no doubt I would be caught eventually. How could I not be? I went haywire and left a bloodbath back there. I'm sure my DNA was somewhere in all that mess at the scene of the crime.

Oh well. I talked to a chainsaw. Maybe that'd get me an insanity plea.

I soon found myself walking through the woods on the outskirts of town, about a mile from where Earl and Joe lay bloody and rotting. The woods were not vast, but not particularly shallow either. There were parts that were so thick they blocked out the sinking afternoon sun and left me wandering in shadows. But the sun shone through in many parts, and Amy seemed to know her way around pretty well, so it wasn't hard to navigate. But I was anxious to kill, and nervous I'd be spotted. A sudden sense of urgency began to flow through me and the itch for action began.

"How much farther, Amy?"

Not far. There will be a clearing in the next few minutes. That will be the place.

I passed into the clearing about six minutes later. Ahead of me was a road with more woods beyond. I stepped onto the concrete and knelt to take some pressure off my back. Amy did not make a light companion.

"So what am I looking for?" I asked her, breathing heavily.

Look to your left.

To my left I saw a long green car parked about twenty feet away on the other side of the road. The radio was playing some folk rock song and there was a lot of smoke rolling out the windows.

"Is that the car I'm looking for?"

Yes.

"And they helped kill you?"

Yes. They kidnapped me and took me to the others.

"Then they'll die today."

It was time to move, time to kill—time to avenge Amy.

I breathed deeply and forgot the pain in my body. The air rushed into my lungs, its crispness invigorating me. I didn't know what time of year it was, but judging by the slight chill setting in, and the orange leaves on the trees, it was autumn—a good season to die.

My feet began to move and I raised Amy into position. I could hear the murmuring and chuckling of the boys floating on the still air. One laugh in particular made me stop. I recognized it and it gave me that feeling of dread that was becoming all-too-familiar.

My knees started feeling weak. This sickening sensation was becoming heavier for me to carry than Amy was and heavier on my mind than the murders. I stood in place and began to wobble, near to falling down.

Are you okay, Sis?

"I don't know."

She was silent for a second.

Can you do this?

"I don't know. I want to. But, it's getting so hard."

Rest for a second. There's a tree to your right. Go lean on it and regain your composure. Sometimes just a few seconds is all you need.

I looked to my right and saw the tall, thick tree about a hundred feet away. I hobbled over to it and set Amy down then leaned against the jagged bark. I actually had a better view of the vehicle from here, and the boys inside were easier to see. The driver looked my way randomly, giving no indication that he'd seen me. He was still laughing. His laugh hurt me. When I saw his face, I remembered him.

Brock. The leader. The kid who gave Joe the bong.

There was another tree closer to their car, and I picked up Amy and crept over to it. It was about fifty feet from them. I crunched leaves as I walked. If not for the radio and the laughter, they would have heard me. But they were too immersed in their own idiocy to notice. When I got as close as I could, standing out of sight behind the tree, I got an even closer look at the driver's face.

I remembered him well. I remembered him laughing aloud as he used a pocketknife to cut the shirt off the woman from the van. I could also see the others in the car and their faces became very clear to me. That's when I fell forward and my face hit the tree.

FLASHBACK III

I then found myself standing in yet another memory I knew wasn't mine. Earl and Joe looked on as the four lowlifes pulled the woman from the van, which remained parked in the same spot from the previous memory when Joe was assaulting her. She still had her clothes on, so apparently he had abandoned his lascivious evil.

"I don't see why I couldn't have a little fun," he said.

"Sawyer wants her in there as soon as possible," Earl said. "Besides, you don't wanna do this stuff out in the open."

"Who the hell's gonna see?"

The boys had her halfway out of the van when she suddenly woke up and began thrashing about. She moaned loud and started kicking her legs and flailing her arms.

"Shit," said Earl. "I told you I didn't give her enough. That's why she kept moaning."

"I'll give her something to moan about," Joe said.

The moronic boys started laughing and calling her every derogatory name stupid, spineless males like to call women to make themselves feel powerful: bitch, whore, slut, cunt—all that meathead bullshit.

"Fuck you," the woman said in a weakened voice. "You guys are gutless cowards. You're not men at all."

Brock let go of one of her legs and swung at her, punching her right in the cheek. This caused the other three to let go of her and let her fall to the ground where they kicked her and cussed at her. Tex got on the ground and slapped her around. Bubba reached for her hair and pulled her up into a sitting position then kicked her in the chest, slamming her back to the ground.

Watching this had me shaking inside. It's not just me, either. The body I inhabited in this dream, or whatever it is, was also trembling with rage. We are of like mind; we want to decimate these deviants. Only what I didn't understand is why this person was with them. Obviously, I could see why he didn't act. He would have been outnumbered. He would have been beaten and killed. That made me remember the vision I had of being strapped to the table by Joe, and that memory only served to confuse the issue more.

Joe stopped the boys and said, "You know what, Earl? I think Sawyer's just gonna hafta wait." He then walked over to the boys and stood beside them. "Git 'er ready fer me, boys."

They all started laughing as they tore off her clothes. The woman began crying for them to stop. The last sounds I heard before I woke back up were her whimpering pleas for mercy, the ripping of fabric, and the gleeful laughter of that evil bastard Brock.

WHAT YOU WANNA DO, AMY?

Starting the chainsaw had become easy; as I approached the pot-smoking jerk-offs, I pulled the starter and ran towards the car. I began with a jog, gathering speed until I was in a full-blown charge. By the time Amy had begun to growl, I was already upon them. Brock jumped and hit the radio, turning it up full blast. Pure Prairie League's "Amie" began blaring across the open air.

As the song rose into the evening sky, I started the slaughter. I came upon the driver-side and yanked open the back door. The tanned kid with the round head, named Bobby Jack didn't know what hit him when Amy's teeth started biting on his neck, slicing his throat wide open and ripping his trachea apart. It only took a few seconds for his head to snap back like a Pez dispenser, the horrid hole in his throat gushing blood.

Bubba, the blond asshole next to him, reached for the door handle, but got nowhere as Amy skewered him in the side, shattering his ribs and burrowing into his chest, churning his heart in her blender. The blade busted through the upper right side of his torso, throwing plump red blobs onto the window next to him. They hit the glass and slid down, looking like flattened beets.

The marijuana vapors mixed with the dust and flesh spit up by Amy's angry claws. Brock, probably in a stoned stupor, had his head halfway turned around, eyes wide, trying to take in the massacre happening to his two deadbeat friends in the back. Tex was already unlocking the passenger side door when Amy slid across the top of the driver's seat and bit down hard into Brock's skull. The song's soft melody played on while he convulsed violently as Amy split his cranium from the ear up. I watched the scalp twist away, as if being sucked into a tornado, to reveal the pale, gleaming skull beneath. Amy sent spider-web cracks all through it, grinding out dust as she busted through its protective shield, leaving the brain exposed. The wrinkled pink slab of meat jiggled and exploded under her mighty attack. I watched with delight as squishy bits leapt up to the ceiling of the car and stuck there, shivering like Jell-O.

I silenced Amy, leaving Crag Fuller to keep singing solo on the radio, and marveled at the masterpiece we had created. The inside of the vehicle was a gory mess. It looked like a miniature slaughterhouse with all the dripping, slithering meat splattered about the interior. We had created art out of a massacre, like a couple of psycho Picassos. The mangled mounds of human carcasses would no doubt put us in the running for the most grisly murder in American history—if only such awards were given!

But the fun wasn't over. Tex had fled the vehicle and was trying to make an escape. He was somewhat husky, so he wasn't fast, and he had stumbled to the ground when he opened the door. I ran around the car in pursuit. He was huffing and puffing as he looked over his shoulder to see where I was.

The setting sun behind me cast my shadow on the ground, and I saw it race before me in the dead, yellow grass. The string-plucking guitar solo ringing out from the car radio for some reason made me run a little faster. I raised Amy high into the air, exhilarated by the kills and the pursuit of the next, and feeling the power of the song pulse through me, as if it had been written just for this moment. My shade was a glorious one, inspiring me to create more mayhem, so I let out a war cry into the still air of the abandoned back road, not caring if anyone else heard me.

Tex didn't make it far into the woods before I caught up with him. Ripping Amy back into action, I swept the back of his legs at the calves. The blow was so precise that the bottom parts of his legs fell off. I severed the right leg first, and it came off clean. The left leg was cut only partway through, and his body managed a couple more steps before the sliver of bone that remained snapped like a stick and sent him tumbling face-first to the ground.

He breathed heavy, unable to speak. Amy turned off once again and I looked at her. The song was still playing in the background, the melodic chorus seeming to talk to me. I held Amy up and looked at her.

"What *do* you wanna do, Amy?"

You already know.

I then smiled and pulled her back into action.

I don't know if Tex intended on pleading for his life, but I didn't give him the chance. As something that resembled a voice seeped from his mouth, I rammed Amy into his right side and began sending her through. I cut across the middle of his back, no doubt pulverizing his kidneys and pancreas and whatever else was stuffed in there. He shook until Amy broke his spine.

When we were done, he looked like a magician act gone bad as his body lay there in two serrated pieces.

When the high of the horror I had visited upon these murdering pieces of trash had worn off, my body felt near to collapse. I turned Amy off and let her drop to the ground, then sat down next to her.

That feeling of liberation was back in me, even though I was at the brink of exhaustion. Those guys were Grade-A scum and needed to be scraped off the streets. However, I couldn't help but second-guess my actions. I mean, massacring six people in one day was a hefty act to carry out, and no doubt came with consequences. Now I felt as though I was waiting for those consequences to come.

I sat there on the roadside feeling sick, ready to vomit then lie down and pass out.

"What have I done, Amy?"

What needed to be done.

"I've killed six people today."

You've killed six monsters.

"I'm not a killer. At least, I don't think I was before. Was I?"

I don't think so, Sis. But, I don't know for sure.

"How could you not know? I'm your sister."

Amy was silent for a few more seconds.

We haven't seen each other in a long time, Sis.

I didn't know what to say. I didn't remember much, but it did feel like Amy and I had been apart for a while. I even wondered how much I truly knew her. She seemed so distant and unreal. I may not have known if she was whom I thought she was, but I was willing to maim for her anyway.

'I don't think I'm a killer, Amy. I mean, I guess I am now. But I don't think I was before."

You're an avenger.

I chuckled. "Sure. That's what I'll tell the judge."

You did what's right. Sometimes doing what's right is illegal. Laws don't exist to protect us or give us justice. Lawyers make laws so they can exploit the system. It's up to us to do what needs doing.

I nodded. "That might be, Amy. But I don't think that's a defense that would hold up in court."

No, you're correct.

"Are we done?"

No. The hardest and most dangerous kill is yet to come.

My heart beat a little more, pounding on my stomach from all the way up in my chest.

"I'm not so sure I like the sound of that, Amy. But then again, I'm not so sure I don't."

After a few more quiet minutes, I rose and picked her up.

"Okay, Amy. Where to?"

CHAPTER FIVE: THE HARDEST KILL

A my took me far away from the hillbilly back roads of this small town into the inner city. I walked a different path through the woods as evening came and went. About a half-hour later, we came out in a completely different area. A broken street next to a railroad track, lined with raggedy shotgun houses, greeted me. It must have been garbage night because trashcans were at the end of every driveway. It was full dark and silent, no one stirring there in the shadows. A few cars drove by a few streets over, but this was definitely a city that sleeps.

"Okay, Amy, where are we going?"

There is an alley behind the house across the street. Walk to it, go all the way down, and turn left.

"You want me to walk through that person's yard?"

Yes. They don't care. Nobody really cares about much out here.

"You do remember that you're a chainsaw and I am carrying you, and both of us are covered in blood, right? That's not the kind of sight people overlook."

No one cares. Trust me. You do *trust me, don't you Sis?*

I did trust her. I walked across the street and followed her directions. After turning left, I came upon a seedy-looking bar at the edge of a parking lot that was even more rundown than the last street. Some country music played from inside, not that modern bubble gum nonsense, but the old kind that evoked images of moonshine stills and cowboy hats. I could smell whiskey from where I stood.

"This is a lovely place," I said.

And it has many patrons. Try to stay out of sight for a moment.

"If anybody sees me, I'll just tell them I got off work at the slaughterhouse. I'm sure that will be enough for these bumpkins."

It might if there was a slaughterhouse nearby. But there's not.

"What about a Kroger's deli?"

The only grocery store around is called Corner Mart and it's about eight blocks away.

"Where are we anyway, Amy? This town sucks."

Yes, it does. There are many bad people in this town.

"I can see that. I'm starting to think my new vocation was well chosen."

This man you are about to confront. He is the most dangerous of all the kills. It will be a huge risk.

"Why?"

Because, in this small town full of bad folk, he is well known and well liked.

"Well that's comforting, Amy. Who is he?"

Amy did not answer me. Instead, about a minute passed before she said anything else.

There he is, coming out of the bar.

I saw a husky man close to six feet tall coming out of the bar. He was bald and he wore a flannel shirt and blue jeans. He had a gun holstered at his hip. That was trouble enough. But what made matters worse was that I knew his face, and it brought about that dread again.

"Amy, it's happening again."

I know. Let it. You must. You have to know.

I breathed heavily and my heart raced. My vision went black once more. I had gone back into the mystery person's past once again.

FLASHBACK IV

I was standing there with the man from the bar, Earl, and another man I recognized vaguely but couldn't quite place. He was a tad overweight and had a pockmarked face. His black hair was slightly long and he had a thick graying mustache. He looked lost in thought as he talked to the man from the bar, who looked serious. Earl was biting the nail of his pointer finger, appearing very concerned.

"I'm telling you Sawyer, that woman is going to make trouble for you," the bar man said to the man with the pockmarked face.

Sawyer? That must have been the boss.

Sawyer sighed and said, "What should I do to shut her up, Hansen?"

Hansen, the man from the bar, shrugged. "I think there's really only one thing you can do. She's pretty upset with you, and she's adamant about exposing you and your operation."

Becoming gravely serious, Sawyer, who loomed over Hansen, said, "If I'm exposed then you'll be exposed."

"Is that a threat?" Hansen wrinkled his brow when he asked.

"No. It's a reminder."

"You think I don't know that?"

"I'm making sure it doesn't slip your mind."

"Like it slipped your mind to not be seen with Brock and his stupid friends?"

"Look Hansen, I already know I fucked up. We all make mistakes. Need I remind you about the drug bust you fucked up last year? Besides, why weren't you at her house to chase Brock away? She wouldn't have recognized him if you would have been there. Since you couldn't show up in time, she got a good look at him and his car. This mistake is on you as much as it is on me, if not more."

Hansen lifted his finger, ready to continue the argument, but Earl stepped in. "Look, no need to fight over this. We all fucked up. I picked a bad mark. She's smarter than your average sucker. If I hadn't picked her, and if Brock had been quicker and more efficient, then neither one of your fuck-ups would matter, and vice versa. We all dropped the ball. Now we have to leave it up to Joe."

For the first time since I started having my visions, the person I was possessing spoke.

"What do you mean, give her to Joe?" It was a man's voice and it sounded familiar.

All three men looked at me. Earl said, "Keep your mouth shut, kid. Don't speak until someone asks you to."

"Hey!" Sawyer said sharply. "Who the fuck are you to bark orders at anybody? Don't talk to him like that. You let me handle him."

Earl looked at the ground and said, "Sorry, Boss."

Sawyer, who was well over six-feet tall and stood next to me, looked at me and said, "You know why we call Joe. Why would you even ask?"

Hansen was watching me, too. That's when I noticed what he was wearing: a dark blue, button up shirt with a front pocket on each breast, and dark slacks to match, with shiny black shoes on his feet. The name patch on his left breast read, 'Hansen'. There were other patches that I couldn't make out. But I could easily make out the shiny tin plate pinned to his shirt. It said 'Sgt. Hansen, APD'.

"Oh shit," I said to myself.

Looking at Sawyer, Hansen pointed at me and said, "Why did you bring him along? He seems a little soft."

Sawyer waved him off. "He's fine. Don't worry."

"You sure?"

The big man's eyes widened and he said more sternly, "End of discussion."

Hansen held up his hands and said, "Fine. You just need to decide what you're going to do about this loudmouth lady. If she starts talking and my superiors start investigating, they might find out some worse shit than the extortion and robbery."

Sawyer sighed. "She's got to go. Can you bring her to me?"

"Not directly. But I can arrange something."

"Then do it, and do it soon."

My vision faded again, and I woke up outside of a parking garage with Sawyer and Earl. Sawyer was on his cell while Earl was talking to me.

"Now, you just stick to the plan and everything will be fine. Don't get out of the car unless there's trouble and don't start driving until you see me leaving. All you are tonight is back up and a set of eyes. Got it?"

"Yeah," my person said.

Sawyer ended his phone call and said, "It's arranged. Hansen told her to meet him here to follow up about her report against us. He told her he was able to dig up some evidence against me. She should be coming here within the hour. Earl, you got the stuff?"

Earl held up a small black doctor's bag and said, 'Right here."

"Good. Make it fucking quick. Joe's already got things set up at his place. Brock's standing by, too. If everybody does what the fuck they're supposed to do, then all will run smoothly and not turn into a hot bucket of piss like last time." Sawyer then looked at me. "You good?"

I nodded.

"We're flushing a big pile of shit tonight. We all stepped in it. So pay attention. Be alert and do what Earl says while you all are in there. If you don't, you'll have to answer to me. Got it?"

I nodded again. The man I was occupying was wrenched with sorrow and boiling with rage, torn between helping this woman and self-preservation. Naturally, he was choosing security, which I imagine most people would have in this dire predicament. Whatever he was doing, and however he got there, he was partially regretting it but partly glad. Deep down inside, discovering these scumbags ignited some strange sense of purpose in him – a purpose that provided a way to fulfill a hunger burning within. I didn't understand it, but I felt it. This rabbit hole seemed to keep getting deeper and I was now feeling that same mixture of regret and purpose from following Amy's voice into the shed and picking her up. What the hell had she gotten me into?

Earl slapped me on the shoulder.

"Okay man, let's go."

Earl took off towards the van I had seen him in earlier, and I followed him and got into the car I was driving in the first vision. One black-gloved hand took hold of the steering wheel while the other turned the key in the ignition. The car started and I followed the van into the parking garage, and faded back into reality.

CITIZEN'S ARREST...SENTENCE AND EXECUTION

I was shaking when I came to, watching Sgt. Hansen smoke a cigarette outside the bar.

"He's a cop," I said.

Yes. A sergeant.

"I can't kill a fucking cop, Amy. That would be taking it too far."

But he's a bad cop, as crooked as they come.

"That doesn't matter, Amy. A crooked cop is still a cop, and other cops will protect him. It's like what you said earlier about lawyers. That's how I feel about cops. They're not here for us; they're here for themselves. I kill a cop, bad or not, they'll come for me, and they won't stop until they get me."

Not if his murder is connected to the murders of the other guys. It will look suspicious having all of them killed in the same night. People will start asking questions and the police will start looking at their victims, or at other outfits. They probably won't even find you.

"That's wishful thinking, Amy. Cops are a brotherhood, a fraternity that watches each other's backs. I can't possibly go this far. You're asking too much."

Sis, you have to do this. It's not just for me that these people must die. Their deaths avenge those they destroyed and protect other people from becoming their victims. This man is the worst of them all simply because he earns the trust of people and then allows them to be extorted, threatened, and assaulted by these bastards. He gained that woman's trust and then led them right to her, and you know what that happened after that. He's supposed to protect the populace, but he protects the gangsters instead because he thinks the city owes him something and the bad guys pay better. He's a lowlife and a danger to the city. You need to end him.

I scratched the back of my head, feeling that scar again. I rubbed the side of my head and felt a larger one there, too. That's when I realized how tender those spots were. It felt like I had stitches in my skull. I wanted to ask Amy why my head had these weird scars, but the issue with Sgt. Hansen seemed more pressing.

"I guess I see what you're saying, Amy. No, I *do* see what you're saying. This man is shit. But how could I kill him and get away with it?"

Don't worry about that, Sis. Just treat him as you did the others: get in there, kill him, and get out.

"The others weren't cops, were they?"

No. But it doesn't matter.

"I think it does, Amy. I can get away with killing civilians. They don't really care about that. But if I kill one of them, they'll never stop."

It doesn't matter, Sis. You're talking in circles. You already said this. Are you trying to get out of this because you're losing your nerve?

"No."

Then do it.

"How? I can't just run at him out here in the open. It's not like the others. There are people around. Help me out."

On the nights he gets off at six, he leaves his car at the station and walks to the bar, drinks for a couple of hours, and walks home. For him to get home, he has to walk all the way down Maria Alley to Cecile Street. That's about a mile and a half. Most of the alley crosses the old business district, which now consists mainly of abandoned shops. About a third of the way down there's a vacant body shop; the old bay is missing its door. The front of the empty shop is wide open. The glass on the windows and door were busted out ten years back and the boards that replaced the glass came down about three years later. You can enter through there, cross the shop, and wait at the bay door for him to pass by.

"Sounds to me like you really have this all planned out, Amy."

That's because I do. I've had a lot of time to think it through.

"But how do you know so much about these people?"

No response.

"Amy? How do you know so…"

Don't worry about it, Sis. I'll let you know soon enough.

"No. If I'm going to kill a cop, I need to know now."

I guess you could say I was kind of close to one of them for a little while. That's all I'll tell you. Trust me when I tell you that if you kill Hansen in the alley, no one will know for a long time. It's dark and the only other people down there are vagrants and criminals and neither one will care about a dead cop. If you leave him alive, more lives will be lost. You are the only one who can stop him. You have the chance right now. Do it.

I looked down at Amy dangling at my side. I looked up at Hansen as he flicked away his cigarette and turned to go back in the bar, blowing the smoke out as he went. I started to contemplate the severity of the situation, weighing the pros and cons of killing him *and* of leaving him alive. It was a tough decision, but in the end, I knew what had to be done.

"Okay Amy. I'm probably going down anyway. I might as well burn down the whole fucking house."

Amy was right. The street was dark and empty. All the shops were empty, no people were in sight, and none of the streetlights worked. This was a real ghost town, at least this section. I guessed there wouldn't have been any witnesses to me killing Hansen. But I was sure the grinding of the chainsaw would echo through the night loud enough for anyone within earshot to hear.

I walked for about twenty minutes before Amy stopped me.

Here it is.

I stood before the body shop looking at the darkness within. The air rolling out into the street stunk like death and shit. I didn't even want to imagine how many animals, or people, died in there. No telling how many people had urinated and defecated inside. Combining that with the weather and age, I was torn between going through with this plan or turning back and killing Sgt. Hansen outside the bar.

But good sense won out and I took a deep breath and walked in. I almost tripped countless times on debris of various types. The interior funk nearly smothered me. Any time I would suck in a breath the rotten smell went into my mouth and down my throat. It was tantamount to swallowing moldy bread soaked in rotten milk. I felt like I could projectile vomit on command.

"You owe me big time, Amy."

She said nothing.

While there were many things bad about this entire situation, the worse was probably that I was literally drifting aimlessly through impenetrable murk. Having had to dodge around junk I kept bumping into, I had lost all sense of direction. I didn't know if I was heading for the bay, or for the adjacent vacated shop, or right back to where I started. I hoped Amy would tell me if I was going the wrong way, but did she even know?

After about fifteen minutes of stumbling around blind, I began to smell the outside and see a faint glimpse of light in front of me. It was moonlight. I could have cried with relief.

"Please tell me this is the bay by the alley, not the front door of another shop."

This is the place.

"Thank the Lord. How long do I have to wait?"

It shouldn't be much longer.

I stood and waited, spending the first few minutes silently working up the nerve to attack when the time came. But working up the nerve only made me more nervous, so I let it slide from my mind and relaxed. Over the next few minutes, I concluded that it was so dead out here that no one would see me kill this son of a bitch. And once I was done, I could just get the fuck out of here and be gone. I didn't know who I was anyway, so I could play the crazy card if I eventually was caught. I now had a plan and I felt pretty good about it.

This newfound elation was soon put on hold as I heard the sound of footsteps coming down the alley. My fingers involuntarily slid onto Amy, ready to start her up and let her rip. This was a good sign. I was not hesitating. My instinct was to kill.

Wait. Is that a good thing?

It's him, Sis. Get ready. Wait until he passes and then attack.

I stepped back into the shadow, just enough to remain out of sight.

The footsteps got closer; soon Sgt. Hansen was in sight. It only took a couple of seconds for him to pass, but it felt like I had been standing there all night watching him move along.

When he passed the door by a few feet, Amy spoke.

Now!

I turned her on and stepped out into the alley. There was just enough moonlight to see by, and I was going right for the crooked cop. The sound of the chainsaw engine caused him to turn almost immediately. He looked at me and said, "What the fuck?"

I jabbed Amy's blade at him and missed. He danced to the side, hitting the brick wall. I swiped her at him again; the blade struck the wall sending sparks flying through the alley like fireflies.

"What the fuck?" he said again, stumbling back.

I thrust Amy at him again but wasn't close enough to hit him. The darkness and the madness made my judgment of distance a little off. He moved to the side, behind something dark lying in the alley, and kicked it at me as hard as he could. The item flew at my legs and I quickly sidestepped. The item flew past me and I moved forward, awkwardly, swinging the chainsaw back and forth at Sgt. Hansen.

He dodged successfully each time, but tripped on something behind him and fell to the ground. Lucky for him, my last swing hit a metal light post in the alley and rattled Amy in my hands, causing me to stop.

This was all that Hansen needed.

He pulled his gun and fired. It was a rushed and nervous shot, so the bullet didn't hit me. But it did hit Amy, knocking her from my hand.

The impact sounded like a homerun swing. The chainsaw rattled and fell to the ground, spinning a few times before dying out.

"Amy!" I yelled.

"What?" Hansen said. "Who the fuck is Amy?"

He stood up and I looked at him, rage racing through me. I gritted my teeth and seethed.

"Christ," he breathed. "You're a fucking junkie, aren't you?"

I kept staring at him.

"I'm so sick of you people. You fucking crackheads and speed freaks and meth maniacs. Some people feel sorry for you, but I don't. You did this shit to yourself. I wish they'd just let me put a bullet in all of you and rid the world of you worthless pieces of shit. I don't know what's worse, the druggies or the homeless. You look like both, which makes you a double shit sandwich. I should just kill you now, you dirty fucking bitch."

Every word that fell from his mouth deepened my rage. I became fully aware of what a deplorable human being he was. The sound of his voice brought back bad memories from that vague and distant place. Boy, Amy was one-hundred percent right all along. In that moment, I regretted ever doubting the deed that needed doing. Sgt. Hansen was an abomination that needed to die, and die horribly.

I knelt down like I was going to pick Amy up. Hansen pointed his gun at me.

"Don't move, dirtbag. You pick that chainsaw up and I'll put your brains through the back of your head."

I slid my hand across the ground, picking up something round and heavy that lay next to Amy. It felt like a doorknob, so that's what I assumed it was. It was heavy, like the old kind, and it fit nicely into the palm of my hand.

I stood up, cupping the knob. He stepped closer, keeping the gun trained on me. I raised my hands.

"You think that's going to save you? You tried to cut me up with a fucking chainsaw. You think I'm going to let someone like you keep walking the streets?"

"What are you going to do, arrest me?" I don't know why I even said that.

He snickered. "Hell no. I wouldn't waste the time and paperwork on you. I'm just going to shoot you and be done with it."

"Oh, are you?"

"Yeah."

"Then why haven't you?"

"Because I like toying with creeps like you, slut. It's what I do."

"How manly of you. You know what I like to do?"

"Probably any drug you can get your hand on, you junkie cunt."

"Not quite."

I threw the knob as hard as I could. He had gotten so close to me that I couldn't miss, and my timing was perfect. My arm shot down like a flash of lightning and the item smashed into Hansen's face with a loud crunching sound. He dropped the gun and both hands went straight to his face. I picked Amy up and sent Hansen hard to the ground with a kick to the chest.

The knob had done more than it needed to. There was a large dark blot of liquid spread across his face. He tried to speak but his voice was garbled. It sounded like his mouth was full of cotton. I stood over him, placing one foot on each side of him and spat on his face. For the first time, I felt like talking to one of these animals.

"You're a real piece of dog shit, Sgt. Hansen. I know who you associate with, those degenerate scumbags in town." I could see his eyes go wide. "Oh yeah, I know all about them. Earl, those four boys, and that rapist Joe. Guess what? They're all dead, courtesy of Amy and me. Oh yeah, and I know what you all did to that woman. And I know what you did to Amy."

Stop talking now, Sis.

I lifted Amy towards my face and said, "But I want him to know I know before he dies."

You've said enough already. Kill him while you have the chance.

"You're right."

I looked down at him again and said, "You never answered my question."

Hansen didn't speak; he just grunted and held his face.

"You want to know what I do?" I then revved Amy up and continued. "I run my own personal slaughterhouse, and I cut up pigs like you."

I lowered Amy to his legs and she bit in with her usual spray of blood. Hansen screamed and I said, "Maybe you should have put a bullet in me and did *yourself* a favor."

His hands came away and I saw the big splatter of blood on his face. I then smiled and said, "How thoughtful of you to give me something to aim for."

Slowly, I pressed Amy towards his face. The tip touched his nose first, cutting it away like butter. Instinctively, he tried to grab Amy, but she destroyed his fingers in seconds. I turned the blade on his hands, cutting them to ribbons. I then moved the chainsaw to the right and cut his left arm off at the shoulder. His right arm was waving around, so I sliced it away as well, just above the elbow. His stumps gushed blood all over the ground.

Next, I moved the blade through his neck and into his chest, decimating everything along the way. I watched his body shudder and his face dance around as Amy tore his throat and chest to shreds. I slowly ran the blade back up to his face, destroying his facial structure and skull. When I felt the blade hit the concrete beneath Hansen's head, I knew there was nothing left. Hansen was beyond suffering now, so why bother. I turned Amy off.

As I stood there in the alley, I relished the new shower of blood and bone that had rained upon me. It baptized me, revitalized me. I was a new woman. I set Amy down and smeared it all over my face and through my hair; I rubbed it into my arms, feeling my thick, hard biceps and triceps bulging from the workout I had just gotten.

"You were right, Amy. I'm sorry I ever doubted you. That man needed to die."

You are beginning to see the truth of the world. Good people are ruled by evil, and one must act evil to end evil.

"Yes, I can see it."

And how does it make you feel to kill evil?

"Righteous. Purposeful. Alive"

Then you believe in what you've done?

"I do. I know it is morally justifiable."

And would you do it again?

I stopped reveling in the moment and thought about what Amy had just asked me, and it disturbed me.

"Why do you ask?"

Because you might have to do it again.

"I killed these men because I knew they were evil. I saw their evil deeds with my own eyes. Any doubts about those visions that I had were erased when I saw the look in Hansen's eyes when I mentioned the others," I said, pointing at Hansen's corpse. "I had no doubt. But I wouldn't dare appoint myself the right to deem someone guilty without knowing it. It would be unwise and as flawed as our current system."

But with proof, you would know it was justified.

"What are you asking me, Amy?"

Again, she was silent.

"What about Sawyer?"

Amy remained silent.

"Then are we done now?"

Go home, Sis. It's time to go back to Dad's.

I sighed. Sawyer was not on my list. He might have already been dead. I didn't ask because I didn't care. I wanted to go home. I didn't think I had it in me to kill anymore, at least not on that night.

"You might need to help me find the way."

CHAPTER SIX: AMY COMES HOME

The trek home was wearisome. Amy and I were covered in blood and body bits. If this weren't such a sparsely inhabited area, the cops would have probably picked us up. Every step of the way I was worried they would. I glanced over my shoulder so much I might have twisted my neck. Thankfully, I never saw any policeman. I only saw two cars: a white Camry that rattled by me so fast I doubted they even saw me in the dark, and a black car I was almost sure was the same black car I saw earlier, only this time the driver didn't slow down and stare. The windows had been up and it drove on past me without incident. I thought that maybe they lived on this street.

It felt like it took hours to get to my dad's house. I walked up the driveway, grungy with gore, and entered the house through the opened side door. There were two decisions before me—return Amy to the shed, shower, and try to cover up my crimes, or tell Dad what I'd done so there'd be no surprises later.

"What should I do, Amy?" I asked as I stood in the doorway.

She said nothing.

"You can't answer me all of a sudden?"

Amy didn't peep—the continued silence hung there. The choice was to be mine. Why not? I would suffer the punishment; Amy was only a chainsaw.

Repercussions were all but a certainty. There was no way I'd get away with it, unless I ran, which I had decided I didn't want to do despite considering it previously. I made my decision. I didn't want to make matters worse. So I sighed and set her down on the kitchen table, where remnants of a solo meal remained, and then pulled out a chair and sat down.

There was a china cabinet against the wall across from me. It had a large mirror inside, and I finally got a look at myself. I got up and walked to the cabinet.

My hair and face were caked in blood. I touched my cheeks, they were fine and my jaw was strong. I was not surprised that I had little problem wielding Amy once I saw my broad shoulders. I remembered the bumps on my head and turned to see the reflection of those I had felt on the side. There was a long, stitched-up scar running along the right side of my head in an arc. I tried to turn to see what was on the back of my head but was unable to get a good look. I then saw a small mirror on the kitchen table, so I picked it up and angled it so the reflection in the china cabinet would reveal the reflection of the back of my head on the tiny mirror. Once I had the correct position, I saw a thin, vertical scar about two inches long towards the base of my skull. Even though I had felt both scars earlier, and despite the mysterious flashbacks I'd been having, finally seeing the scars caused me alarm.

"What happened to me, Amy?"

She still did not answer me.

"Now you have nothing to say?"

Apparently, she did not, because silence continued to reign. I sighed and sat back down at the table. I guessed she was done with me since I had completed her revenge. I wanted to be mad at her but couldn't. Maybe her spirit had left the chainsaw, her purpose now fulfilled. Or maybe my hallucination was over.

The TV in the living room was on, but not too loud. I called out, "Dad! I got something to tell you."

The TV suddenly went quiet, but no reply came. I breathed in and out for a second and said, "Hey Dad, I got something to tell you. Can you come in here?"

I would have gone to him, but I didn't want to track blood across the floor. I heard the sound of a recliner's footrest slamming shut, the metal twang echoing in the living room. Rapid heavy footsteps rushed towards the kitchen, shaking glassware. I kept my head down, not wanting to look my father in the eyes. The footsteps stopped behind me and I braced myself for his exclamation.

And he exclaimed all right, only his words were not what I had expected.

"Who the fuck are you?" he yelled.

I turned around and gasped, then immediately stood up and backed away. I was looking at a familiar face: a man with semi-long black hair and a graying mustache, overweight, and with a pockmarked face. Sawyer's mouth hung open in shock, and as I looked into his dark eyes, I realized I recognized him more than I thought in the flashback.

"I thought this was my dad's house," I said.

Sawyer backed away, eyeballing my bloodstained clothes and throwing glances at Amy dripping on the table. When he looked me in the eyes, a look of knowing started to show on his face.

"Wait a second," he said and smiled. "Dad, huh? Well, you do look an awful lot like him. He looked a lot like his mother, too. It's a damn shame he fucked up like he did."

I had no idea what he meant. But when I looked around the house, it became more and more familiar. Except for Amy. When I looked at her lying on the table, she looked less like an entity and more like a plain old chainsaw. But, I could still feel that other presence in my head. It just wasn't talking.

"I know you," I said.

Sawyer nodded. "I bet you do."

"What did you do to Amy?"

Sawyer squinted and looked confused. "What are you talking about?"

"Amy. What did you do to her? I know it was you. I saw what you did to the other woman. I saw you and your friends." I began to feel the anger rise in me again, not just from *my* heart, but also from the heart of another.

Sawyer's face went from amused and confused to very stern. "What do you mean?"

"I mean Earl, those boys, the cop, and that rapist Joe. I saw all of you. I know all about you."

"Tommy sent you didn't he? You tell that little bastard I'm gonna find him and finish the job."

Tommy? Who was that?

Amy? Tommy? Sis?

Me?

"I don't know who sent me," I said. "But you see all this blood on me? That's your whole crew right there. Every one of them. Even that crooked son of a bitch, Hansen. Now, there's only one of you left."

With shock now on his face, Sawyer asked, "You killed every one of them? Even Hansen?"

"You're goddamn right I did."

His face then changed. He now looked impressed. "That's some pretty good killin'. Too bad your brother wasn't as good as you."

"My brother?"

He laughed. "Don't play dumb. No sense in protecting Tommy. I'm gonna get him sooner or later. It's just unfortunate you didn't come along first, or I wouldn't have to do what I'm about to do."

I looked at Amy, or whatever that chainsaw was (just a chainsaw?), ready to grab her if Sawyer came after me. I began to feel warmth from her, as if I wasn't alone. Whoever was in my head began to come back.

"Where am I, Amy?" I asked.

"Why do you keep talking to yourself? Did you go crazy on me, girl?"

Where you are doesn't matter, Sis.

"Amy, what's going on? Who is he?" I began to feel panic. Bad memories were coming back.

Sawyer had begun to come forward, but stopped when I made a move for the chainsaw.

Do you not remember?

My body started to shake. Numbness tingled in my feet and began to spread upward. My vision was darkening again and I blacked out. But before drifting into unconsciousness, I said, "Don't let him get me, Amy."

I won't.

It was the last thing I heard before slipping away.

FLASHBACK V

I was sitting at the same kitchen table where I had laid Amy. It was just Sawyer and me. He was smoking and talking, but I couldn't hear him. The ringing that was in my ears drowned out all other sound. It took a little bit for it to subside. As I watched and waited to hear the conversation I was apparently involved in, all seemed to move in slow motion.

"Do you have a problem with the operation we run here, Tommy?" I heard Sawyer ask when my hearing returned.

"Not at all."

"Good, because we have a good thing going. Nothing goes on in this town that we don't get a piece of. Sometimes we have to get into some heavy shit. I don't mind bringing you in, but I need to be sure that you'll do what I need you to do. The others are a little worried about me bringing you in, so I'm taking a chance on you. Don't screw me."

"I won't," Tommy (I) said.

Sawyer smiled, apparently satisfied with the answer. Then he said, "I'm really glad you found me, son. At first, I was worried. But now I think it's a good thing."

"Well, I'd been looking for a long time."

The smile faded from Sawyer's face and he looked at the ashtray in front of him. He started butting his cigarette out and sighed. "Look, I could sit here and make excuses for why I never came and saw you all after your mother ran off with ya, but I ain't got one. She left and that was that. I never hated her for it. I understood. She left because she wanted out of this life; she wanted to keep you all away from it. That's what she wanted, so I let her have it. I reckon I could have given up the life, but the truth is I didn't want to. It just is what it is."

"I got it, Dad."

"Well, like I said, I'm glad you found me. Whatever happened to your sister?"

Tommy shrugged. "Mama sent her to live with Grandma. She decided she couldn't take care of us both not long after leaving you. About a year later, I went to Uncle Drayton's. She stayed gone for years, came back and found me about five years ago."

"What about your sister?"

"She never found her. Sis ran away when she was twelve and no one in the family ever heard from her again."

Sawyer nodded and said, "Well, it's just as well. If she turned out to be anything like your mother, we're better off. You're not like your mama, though. You're tough, like me."

Tommy scoffed. "Like you? Tougher, more like it."

The two of them had a laugh and the vision ended and gave way to a new one.

In this vision, I wasn't Tommy. I was me. I could feel it. I was on a swing set in my backyard and I was really young. God, I must have been three or four, maybe five at the oldest. I was very upset, crying. The face of an angry man was about six inches from my face, yelling and cussing at me.

"Stop crying, you fucking little bitch! You're just a fucking crybaby like your mother! The worst mistake I ever made was fucking that dumb cunt because she gave birth to you!"

The man was more familiar to me than he was earlier today when I remembered this. He was young, probably in his mid-twenties. His hair was long and black, and he had a mustache. He wasn't overweight yet but he still had the pockmarks.

"Oh my God," I said to myself, feeling my stomach fill with barf.

Sawyer...he was—is—my...

"Sawyer!" A broad-shouldered black-haired woman came running through the backyard, looking angry. Sawyer turned around to face her.

"What the hell do you want?"

The woman pushed past him and picked me up off the swing.

"My God, Sawyer, she's just a baby. Don't you dare take your anger at me out on her."

"Then you should be out here watching her. I got shit to do."

"She's your daughter, you asshole. You should want to be out here with her."

Through the eyes of a child, the backyard was enormous. But I could tell it was actually quite small. There was a little boy playing in a dirty sandbox on the other side of it. He was digging away with his purple plastic shovel, not really doing anything, and glancing up at us every few seconds.

"I got things to do," Sawyer reiterated.

"Nothing you do should be more important than your family. I don't care how you feel about me. But you should love your children."

"Loving children is women's business. Making money to feed the fuckers is a man's."

"You disgust me."

I started crying again. Their anger was too much for me. Sawyer let loose his rage right away.

"Goddamnit! Is that all she ever does is cry?"

"She's a child, Sawyer. Children cry. What the hell is wrong with you?"

"You don't fucking hear Tommy crying all the time."

52

"Tommy is three years older than her, and he used to cry quite a bit. Why don't you act like a father and hold her?

"I got better things to do."

My mother shook her head and said, "You're a piece of shit."

Sawyer grabbed her arm and yanked it. "Hey! Don't you fucking call me that. I put those kids in you. It was my seed that made them."

"Oh whatever. You think that means something? They grew in *my* body. Any male can spurt that nasty shit into a woman. That goo doesn't mean anything until it makes it to the egg. You're just a fucking donor. Now fuck off you worthless bastard."

Sawyer's face turned red and he quickly backhanded Mom. It caused her to take a few steps back but otherwise didn't faze her. It only made her mad.

"And you're a coward to strike me while I'm holding my daughter."

He then grabbed her by the shoulders and shook her. "I ain't no coward, you whore! And fuck that little bitch you got in your arms. Don't get mouthy while you're holding her and she won't be in danger."

"You're no man," she said as her head snapped back and forth. "You're a pig. A dog. A spineless fucking snake."

Sawyer yelled something unintelligible and threw Mama to the ground. I heard Tommy scream, "Mama!"

I rolled from my mother's arms and started crying again. Sawyer went to grab me and said, "I'm gonna shut this bitch up for good!"

"No!" Mama cried and jumped to her feet. "Don't you fucking touch her you sick son of a bitch!"

And with that, she punched Sawyer in the face, sending him crashing to the ground. She stood in front of me and said, "You'll have to walk over my corpse first."

Sawyer jumped up and tried to tackle my mom, but she grabbed a hold of him and stood her ground. She was strong, apparently stronger than he was, and she managed to force him away and shove him to the ground. He jumped up and tried to slap her but she moved and punched him in the face again, knocking him back on his ass.

He sat there holding his cheek as she pointed at him and said, "I'll let you get away with a lot of the bullshit you do to me, but I will fucking die before I ever let you hurt Amy!"

And that's when the vision ended and I snapped awake.

AMY RISING

"Amy?" Sawyer said. "What are you doing?"

I noticed I was holding Amy in my hand. But, it wasn't Amy. It was just a chainsaw and nothing more. The voice…that wasn't my sister. I didn't have a sister. I had a brother, his name was Tommy, and he used to call me Sis, just like the voice in my head. He had always called me that when we were little kids, before we were separated.

But how? How was he talking to me? Was he talking to me?

"Look," Sawyer said. "You'd better take your crazy ass out of here, or you'll go the same route Tommy did."

Sis, Dad is one of the men that killed me. He organized the whole thing. You have to kill him.

I lifted my head quickly and looked at Sawyer. His eyes were hard and mean. I knew the voice was telling the truth. I turned the chainsaw on. The man screamed and retreated to the living room. I followed, holding the weapon out before me. Sawyer backed away slowly and I came in slower, prolonging his fear.

"What are you doing?" he cried.

"I'm gonna shut a little bitch's mouth for good," I said with a bloody grin.

"Look, we can talk about this."

I thrust the chainsaw forward and he jumped back. His legs hit the couch behind him and he fell into a seated position with his hands up. He then began to plead.

"Look Amy, I'm sorry for leaving you guys. I'm sorry about Tommy, but I had to do what I had to do."

He lies. End his filthy, lying mouth, Sis.

"Oh, don't worry. I will."

I ran the blade along Sawyer's right knee, cutting straight into the bone. He leaned his head back, stretched his mouth open as far as it would go, and wailed. I wasted no time in granting the voice's command. I lifted the weapon and thrust the blade right into Sawyer's mouth.

The inside of his mouth was cut to ribbons. His cheeks split apart, his tongue was ground into pieces, and the rest of his oral cavity became a crimson, meaty stew. I laughed as his teeth shattered and jumped out of his mouth. His face bounced side to side until everything above the mouth disconnected and spun off through the air like a top. The head chunk slid along the wooden floor before stopping in the corner beside the front door.

I turned the chainsaw off and the voice went quiet again. I stood there listening to the silence, considering what all I had just seen and heard. Though the chainsaw was not talking to me, there was most certainly a voice in my head.

"Who are you?" I asked the voice.

Who do you think I am?

"You're not Amy."

No. I am not.

"Tommy?"

Yes, Sis.

Tears began to swell in my eyes. All along, I had recognized his voice. It was my big brother.

"How, Tommy?"

Man, it's a good thing you just killed Dad, Sis. You know how he gets when you cry.

I couldn't help but to laugh, even if the joke was in the poorest taste possible at that moment.

"You can't get out of answering my question now. What's going on?"

It's very complicated, Sis. I don't know how to begin to tell you. To be honest, I'm not even sure I remember it all.

"You have to tell me something, Tommy. I just went on a rampage for you. I mean, I committed patricide for fuck's sake."

Well, at least that was for the greater good.

"I don't deny that. But how are you talking to me? Am I crazy?"

No. You're not crazy. There is some weird shit going on here. But, I can tell you that I am truly dead. At least my body is. I do know that much.

I cried some more. "That's not much comfort."

You're telling me.

"Can you at least tell me what happened to you?"

I got a dark past, Sis. I did some bad things.

"So have I."

Very true. But my memory is hazy. That's why the visions were so clipped. Something has messed up my brain.

"Well, we got to find out what is going on."

I know. I just don't know how.

Just then, there was a knock on the front door. I froze and I could feel Tommy tense up inside me.

"Who is that, Tommy?"

I don't know.

Another knock. Then a voice from outside said, "Amy, please open up."

I looked at the door as if it was the one speaking to me. A third knock came and I found myself walking to the door. I opened it up and saw a man in glasses and a black baseball cap on the porch, smiling at me. The black car I'd seen earlier was parked in the driveway behind him. The man looked like a complete slob, but his eyes were intelligent, even a little crazy.

"Hello Amy. My name is Dr. Nahon. I believe I can answer your questions."

CHAPTER SEVEN: AMY CHAINSAW

I remember him.

"As you should, Tommy," Dr. Nahon said.

"How did you hear him?" I asked.

"With this." Dr. Nahon pulled an earbud from his ear and handed it to me.

I looked it over. It just looked like an old-style hearing aid from the 90s. I held it back out to him and said, "I don't understand."

"Tommy, I think you can remember."

Dr. Nahon put the bud back in his ear.

I remember pieces, but not all.

"I will help you remember so you can show her."

Please.

Nahon reached into his pocket and clicked something. I blacked out immediately.

THE FINAL FLASHBACK

A montage of murder happened before my eyes. They were Tommy's eyes. He was killing people, cutting them up, slitting their throats, setting them on fire, drowning them, strangling them, and even shooting them. I was horrified. I could still feel Tommy and he was unmoved.

"Oh my God, Tommy, you did this?"

Yes. I am a serial killer, Sis.

"Since when?"

I made my first kill when I was nineteen. Some guy who was sexually abusing his girlfriend. I hunted him down and beat in his head with a hammer. Since then, I've killed fifty-seven people. But I don't pick my victims at random. I pick people who I know have done bad things.

"Tommy, that still doesn't make it right."

The montage continued as we spoke. Scenes of bloodshed and lifeless eyes drifted around us like several floating movie screens. Images of Tommy cutting up bodies, burying them, throwing them in rivers, and cremating them tore at my eyes.

Maybe not. But I've always had the urge to kill, even when we were kids. I wanted to kill Dad. I wanted to kill kids at school. I wanted to kill teachers and aides. I just wanted to end life. I knew it was an abhorrent urge. I knew it was wrong. But I couldn't stop it. I needed to see blood. I needed to see the life drain from someone's eyes. But I still had a shred of humanity inside me, and that kept me from picking someone at random and killing them. So I started killing bad people.

"Like murderers and rapists?"

Yes, but not just violent criminals. I killed thieves, liars that hurt people with their lies, identity thieves, corrupt policemen, people that abused animals, people that got other people fired out of spite, bosses that fired people out of spite, people that ruined people's characters for no good reason. I killed these people because they are cankers on society.

"Is that why I felt exhilarated after killing them?"

I don't think so. I don't know. That could have been because of me. Or it could just be in our genes. Dad was a violent fuck, so we both might be.

"What do you mean it could have been because of you?"

The vision soon switched. Tommy was in a jail cell. He had a patch over his eye and he looked very ill. Dr. Nahon was talking to him.

"You won't beat it, Tommy. Your heart is bad. You might have another three years left if you're lucky."

"And you say if I agree to do this, then she'll live?"

"I don't know for certain, but I believe we can make it work. And if we do, it will be a medical breakthrough the likes of which has never been seen. It can be one-step closer to prolonging human life. It might even one day lead to the possibility of immortality. All you have to do is sign the papers."

"You know I want those assholes dead. They need to be dead. They're going to hurt more people,' Tommy said.

Nahon's face changed from eager and ecstatic to anxious. "I know. I have an idea for that. But it's radical and it might not take. If it works, it will be revolutionary. If it does not, then I won't be able to grant that request. But if we wait any longer, then your sister will be the one to die."

Tommy sighed. "Okay. I'll do it."

"Wait," I said. "What is going on here? Why is Tommy like that? And what do you mean his sister will die?"

The vision faded and switched again. Tommy had been beaten up and tied down on the table. Sawyer, Earl, and Joe stood over him. Joe had the blowtorch in his hand. Sawyer looked cruel but slightly disappointed.

"Why'd you do it, Tommy?" he asked.

"Because you bastards deserve to die. You're bad people. You didn't need to kill that woman."

"That woman wasn't going along with the plan, and she was going to talk when she found out we were taking her for all she's worth. If she started talking and the police started looking, then that would be it. I thought you understood that, son."

"I understand you're an evil fuck. And you are all cowards."

Joe laughed. "Well, since you're so courageous, I'll make sure to turn the pain meter up as high as I can. We'll see how tough you really are."

Earl looked at Sawyer. "You sure you want to do this?"

Sawyer shrugged. "He knows too much, and he was going to kill us. Hell, he almost killed *you*. What choice do I have?"

"I know, but does he have to die like this? You know how bad Joe can be."

Sawyer looked down at Tommy and shrugged. "Make an example of him. If I'll do it to my own son, what will I do to other people who cross me?"

"Makes sense to me."

The vision faded in and out, moments of Joe's beastly torture upon Tommy flashed along. We came to with Tommy lying on the table alone in the room. Joe was nowhere in sight. After much struggling, Tommy managed to break the binds on his wrists. They were just straps and not very strong. It was not hard to tear away those on his ankles. He managed to get away and go to the police. But they were already onto him for some other murders. Tommy soon found himself arrested, tried, and imprisoned for life, and no one was listening to his stories about Sawyer's gang.

"What was wrong with your heart?"

I had a bad heart condition. I got it from Mom. She passed away from heart failure not long after I found her. I was fading quickly. I just wanted to see Dad's group of thugs slaughtered. But no one was going to bring them to justice because of Hansen. So when Dr. Nahon came to me with his news, I was ready to listen.

The vision switched to Dr. Nahon entering Tommy's cell. After sliding the bars shut, he took a seat on the bunk across from my brother.

"Tommy, do you remember your sister?"

"Amy? Sure I do."

"Well, she's been in a serious automobile accident. She's suffered severe brain damage. It looks like she won't make it."

Tommy started to cry softly. He might not have seen me in years, but he still cared. I could feel his sorrow and for a brief second, it made me feel loved, which was a feeling that seemed foreign to me.

"But there might be a way to save her."

"How?"

"It's a slim chance, and it's something untested on humans."

"Well, what is it?"

"A brain transplant."

Tommy scoffed. "Yeah, right. Get the fuck out of here with that crackpot bullshit."

"It is something some of us have dedicated our lives to, Tommy. Perfecting a brain transplant would be a monumental discovery. If we could do that and then learn to make artificial brains that can sustain life, we might be able to eradicate death."

"Eradicate death? That's impossible."

"Nothing is impossible. It is actually very possible. We just have to find the right pieces and put them in the right places."

"Have you ever tried it?"

"Not on humans. But we have managed to make it happen with apes and pigs, both of which are similar to humans."

"Let me guess. You're asking for my brain?"

Nahon nodded.

"Why me? Why now?"

"We finally got the okay to do it. Just like with anything else, the wheels turn slowly if they move at all—a lot of bureaucracy. You know. But we now have permission *and* the equipment we need to give the experiment a shot."

"Okay, so let's say I agree to this, would it be her life you're saving or mine? It would be *my* brain in *her* head, so would the memories be mine?"

"We think so. But we don't know. There are some beliefs that memories and instincts are not solely stored in your brain. The theory of genetic memory has touched this subject."

"Well, I don't know what that means. But, would she then have the same urges and impulses to kill that I do?"

Nahon shifted in the bunk and crossed his arms.

"I don't know. Maybe. Maybe not."

They continued to talk and the vision faded out.

WHO IS AMY CHAINSAW?

I re-entered reality back in the living room where my father's corpse lay without its scalp—and part of its skull, and most of its face. The doctor was smiling, like he couldn't even see the carnage.

"Needless to say, Tommy agreed to it," he said. "But his insistence that your father's crime ring be destroyed, and his question as to whether or not you would have his killer impulses, intrigued me. The transplant was a success. And it got me to pondering many things. I decided to put this chip in to track you and record your memories, so to speak."

"Record my memories?" I said. "You really are nuts, aren't you?"

Nahon smiled sheepishly. "Maybe I am a tad. But your memory *can* be recorded. Only in waves and neurons, but that can be read and interpreted, and the data could prove invaluable."

"So, what are you saying? Tommy's brain and mine are fused? Is that why I keep hearing his voice?"

Nahon smiled. "Not exactly. You see, your brain is gone, no more. Dead. You are living with Tommy's brain inside your skull. You hear his voice because it's his brain. But, the intriguing part is that you still have access to your memories."

"So, why did I end up here, in Tommy's world?"

"Because I put you here, and I put the chainsaw in the shed. Once I realized Tommy's consciousness still lived, I convinced him to go along with that crazy story I concocted. I pointed out that he might be able to convince you to kill Sawyer and his gang. I guess it wasn't that crazy of a story, after all. I just put a twist on the part about the two of you being separated. Instead of it being you and Tommy, I had you thinking you had a lost sister named Amy."

Nahon looked insanely satisfied with himself. His eyes shone with something that bordered on lunacy. He was getting high on his own perceived brilliance. I didn't think he was brilliant. I thought he was just a fucking asshole.

"So tell me, Doctor: Why the big story? Why not just tell me the entire truth from the get-go? Why did you go to such great lengths to toy with my fucking life?"

His eyes lost that crazy luminescence for a moment. "I understand how it must make you feel. But *you* must understand the implications of this entire experiment. Preserving your life with a brain from another human being was a success. That alone is a revelation. But I wanted to see if embedding Amy into your new brain would trigger memories of yourself—memories that your brother couldn't possibly have."

"Well, I hate to burst your bubble Doc, but I don't remember a goddamn thing about my life that Tommy wasn't a part of."

Nahon smiled. "Why, of course you do. Some neuroscientists, such as me, believe that each individual has their own unique pattern of brainwaves. Just a little while ago, I read brainwaves that were not like Tommy's. They were like yours. I was unable to learn much about your brainwaves before you died, but I was able to capture something. Now, I've been seeing different patterns pop up briefly throughout the day. I was not sure they were yours, but I knew they were different from Tommy's. That's why the murder was so important. Tommy's brainwaves were clearly dominant during those violent acts, but with each kill, the brainwaves that differed from his got stronger. None of them matched the limited information I had of yours, until a little bit ago. What I just read, only a few minutes before I knocked on the door, was a perfect match to the pattern I collected from your brain about ten minutes before you died. Something in there was a memory from Amy's mind, not Tommy's"

"But when? Tommy was present in every memory I had."

When you remembered Mom and Dad fighting, you also remembered me. You saw me playing in the sandbox. I might have been there, but that was your memory, from your perspective. Amy still exists inside you, Sis.

I nodded, astonished at this madness. It all sounded like bad sci-fi bullshit to me, but Tommy was right. That was *my* memory, not his. The doctor was correct in saying it was amazing. But, it still didn't quell the trembling need to destroy him that was itching to get out of me.

"So, all this time I've been nothing more than a puppet for your project?"

"I wouldn't say you're a puppet. That chip in your head allows me to control your mind to an extent. I can't make you behave certain ways, nor can I control your actions or thoughts. But I can wake you up and make you sleep. I can even help you access memories in Tommy's brain. But I don't know how to get to yours. Your memories must be stored in your genetics, because they are very much alive and present."

"So you put me here with that fucking chainsaw to see if Tommy could make me kill?"

"I wanted to see if you would follow Tommy's urges completely, or if there would even be a trace your own. I needed to read your brainwaves. I wanted to know if Amy still existed. She does, very much so. Even more so than I hoped. She's not just lingering in there somewhere, she is still who she always was. I'm standing here talking to her now."

I swear fire ignited in my eyes. That ridiculous skeletal grin on the doctor's face melted away like candle wax when I looked at him.

"What the hell have you done to me?" I asked.

Now he started to stammer. "Well, I, uh, Tommy wanted those men dead, so I thought it would be the perfect opportunity to see how his brain would work in your body. I wanted to know what you would do. Would you kill like Tommy, or would you try to find Amy's home? You appeared to be stuck between the life of Tommy and the world of Amy. Like I said, it was amazing."

"Amazing?"

"Yes. Why, you're a scientific anomaly, Amy. You could be a key to man's greatest scientific breakthrough. I just need to test you a little bit longer."

"I'm not your fucking lab rat, you asshole!" I yelled, battling back the urge to pummel this weaselly prick.

"Well, uh, hold on now. I just wanted to help you, to help mankind." He backpedaled as I moved closer, clutching the chainsaw tighter and tighter. "Please understand that you were as good as dead, Amy. I put Tommy's brain into you and you took on his instincts and memories while maintaining your own. I tested you to see if you would kill, and you did, but you also remembered Amy, even if incorrectly at first. You still remembered who you are and what you'd been through. It was still there, or else I wouldn't have been able to access any of it. When you went off to kill those men, I knew everything was a success."

"You mean you turned me into a fucking serial killer for some theory?"

"No, not just a theory," he kept talking, but the chainsaw quickly came to life in my hands. I was becoming proficient at wielding it. "Amy, this was not just a theory," he started to yell over the roar of the blade. "It's a miracle. It could cure so much for mankind in the..."

I can't say for sure. But I imagine the last thing Dr. Nahon saw was my face contorting in rage as I brought the chainsaw up in sweeping arc, chopping off his head in one quick bloody motion. The chainsaw was off before his head and body hit the floor.

"You should have fucking let me die!" I screamed at his corpse.

I sat down on the couch, breathing heavily. Tommy and I were both silent for a few seconds. I could feel his anxiety. I had killed the only person who knew what was really going on with us. Dr. Nahon was the only person who could fix this...or end this.

Sis...

"So what's your story, Tommy? Why were you with Dad and all those killers?"

At first, Tommy did not answer me. I became angry. I wasn't letting him off this time.

"Don't you do that! Don't you fucking go silent on me. You owe me this answer, and if you don't give it to me, I will turn this goddamn chainsaw on my skull and end this shit show for both of us."

I suppose I do owe you that much.

"Yes…you do."

It's a simple answer, really. I recall it well, now. I had searched for years for all of you—Mom, Dad, you—and when I found Dad, I discovered he was a scam artist, thief, drug dealer, murderer, and human trafficker. That woman you saw in the flashbacks—her name was Joy Martin. Dad had her going on some insurance scam or something, and was stealing her money and identity. I don't know the details of the scam, but they all fucked up some staged break-in at her home and she found out what was going on. She decided she was going to bring them down. I think you can piece together the rest of that story. After what they did to her, I decided I was going to kill them all, but I got caught. You know the rest from there.

I wiped my eyes. My brother was a sick serial killer, and my Dad was a complete monster. But what was I?

"I can't believe you got me into this, Tommy."

I'm sorry, Sis. I had no idea it would come to this.

"It's not your fault. You were only trying to help. It's twisted fucks like this guy that ruin everything for everybody."

Yes, but I hoped you would finish my work for me. That was wrong of me.

"Oh well. C'est la vie. What the hell can I do about it now?"

What do you plan to do next?

"I don't know. I guess I got the urge to kill now, and I have the expert's brain in my head. Maybe it's time to seek a little revenge on the assholes that did this to me."

Sis, you already killed Nahon. He was the head of it. There's no reason to kill those who worked for him. They were just following orders.

"Yeah, so were the Nazis. But maybe we can find someone who can fix this."

What's to fix?

"No offense, Tommy, but I'd rather be dead than be constantly driven to kill. Ever since we started this, the need has gotten worse and worse. I just murdered that peckerhead like nothing, and I feel no remorse about it. I can't live like this. I'm afraid I'll start killing innocent people just to satisfy the urges."

I understand. But, he had all the details. He'd probably be the only one to fix it, and you killed him.

"Surely he has files or something. None of these eggheaded douchebags can keep themselves from documenting their greatness. I thought he was going to orgasm from just talking about it. The answers have to be out there. I also want to know who I really am and where I come from. We got a lot to figure out and a long road to walk. So, let's start walking. Maybe we can kill a few scumbags along the way."

That sounds like fun, Sis.

I looked down at Nahon's headless body, and his severed head lying next to it. He wondered what I would do. He wondered who I was. I guess I showed him. And I intended to show anyone else who cared to come knocking.

I started walking across the room.

What are you doing, Sis?

I stopped in front of the plain white wall and turned the chainsaw on. Now that I had my answers, I started carving my name into the plaster, maneuvering my weapon with the grace of an ice sculptor. Paint and drywall hit me in the face, and I cut loose some nails and tacks from the wood. I even chopped a beam or two, but not enough to collapse the wall. I cackled as I cut, remembering my name, or at least my nature, which gave me a name of its choosing.

When I was finished, I walked over to the headless doctor and pointed at the wall behind me. "That's who the fuck I am, you son of a bitch!"

I stormed out the door and off into the quiet world before me. The neighborhood was dark, no streetlights and not even any porch lights, so I ventured into the night with my brother's brain in my head and a new name on my lips. The chainsaw wasn't alive. It was just an object. With the new name came a new persona. I was now an enraged, blood-loving, chainsaw-wielding killing machine who had two people living in one body. I wanted to change that. I wanted to be normal. But I also wanted to know where I came from.

For now, at least, I know who I am. I am the name I carved into my dead dad's living room wall just before I walked out of his house, and anyone that came to investigate would know my name, too.

I *am* Amy Chainsaw.

STREET CHEESE

The dingy black Subaru stopped a couple of feet from where Gordy sat under the overpass. The vehicle was speckled with white spots and smelled like rotten milk. Even Gordy, who couldn't recall his last bath, found it repugnant. He stopped chugging his PBR and threw down the can, then stood up to get a better look at the visitor. The other bums that dwelled beneath the roaring freeway took notice and began to investigate the happening. Very rarely did a vehicle not containing a police officer stop in their squalid patch of the city.

When the tall, ghastly man in black emerged, all of them began licking their lips, for in his hands, he brandished a large, white pizza box smelling of Italian sausage and hot, fresh cheddar and mozzarella cheeses. But, Gordy reacted differently. Although the aroma of the freshly cooked pie made his stomach grind like rabbits fucking, the sight of the visitor chilled him to shivers. Something about him was unsettling—an air of darkness much more pungent than the alluring meal he waved around.

The hideous man stood close to seven feet tall, but was skinny as a rake. Clad all in black, with wild white hair puffing out of his driving cap, he cast a haunting image in the blazing sunlight. It was already sweltering where the homeless dwelled, the area bowled in by a ring of concrete, but Gordy was almost certain the temperature rose when this phantom-like character stepped from the car.

His ghoulish face grinned green-teeth and blackened gums as he looked around at the rabble before him. Gordy expected him to start singing, "God is in His Holy Temple" any second. But, he simply held out the box and pulled back the lid, unveiling the culinary masterpiece within.

"You bums want a slice of this?" he called out in a raspy voice.

A bevy of vagrants scuttled towards him, fingers and hands rubbing together, ready to feast. There were six derelicts besides Gordy. He didn't really know any of them and didn't care to. He was planning to drift to somewhere else tomorrow. The exit ramps down there mostly had stingy people unwilling to help the homeless. Most of the time, they ignored him and looked ahead. On occasion, someone might roll down their window and tell him to get a job. He often wanted to reply, "Know anyone that will hire someone without a home address, asshole?" but he didn't. Homeless people causing a ruckus were usually jailed, which didn't bother some, but Gordy liked his freedom, no matter how unrewarding it had always been.

The vagabonds stormed the phantom, ready to rip the pizza from him like a horde of zombies. He yelled, "Act civil, you turds! There's plenty for you all. This is the best pizza you'll ever have. I promise. After you've eaten a piece, you'll never be the same. Why, you'll practically melt with joy!" He followed that with a loud, maniacal laugh while passing out slices to all the hungry hobos.

All except for Gordy, who really didn't like this peculiar development. There was something Janus-faced about that man. No one gave the homeless anything around there, especially not something as beautiful as that hot, fresh pizza. The best they could hope for was cheap, wasted beer and the scraps of discarded food the underpass pigeons and alley cats didn't scarf down first. Adding to that the ominous spectacle the creep was altogether, Gordy opted to dig through the next dumpster he found and pass on the pizza.

But, his shameless neighbors didn't. They voraciously wolfed down the offering, smacking and licking their lips, sucking their fingers like cock-teases, trying to slurp up every sauce glob they could get. One pathetic asshole even got down on his hands and knees to lap it up after a piece of the cheese slid off his slice and hit the ground. Gordy felt pity for them. Even without the disturbing comportment of the Pizza-pie Man, Gordy would still not act so base, so vile—so animalistic. He might have been homeless, but he had some dignity. He was not a savage.

After those around him had their slices, the Pizza-pie Man turned his black eyes to Gordy and said, "What about you, scuzzbucket? There are two pieces left." He picked one up and held it out. "Aren't you hungry?"

Gordy felt something pulling him as he stared at the man, whose face seemed to grow large enough for his mouth to consume Gordy. He laughed and his breath smelled of pizza and decomposition. As the Pizza-pie Man grew nearer, the slice of pizza hovered before Gordy, trying to force its way into his chops. It hit Gordy's tongue and sent an acidic shockwave through his mouth. Reality returned—the Pizza-pie Man's head shrank back to a normal size, and he was standing right in front of Gordy, trying to shove the pizza down his throat. Gordy jumped back when he realized what was happening.

"No!" he yelled, and everyone looked at him.

Smiling, the Pizza-pie Man said, "What's the matter, Gordy? Aren't you hungry?"

Gordy only shook his head. The Pizza-pie Man continued to smile.

"Come on, Gordy. This is the best pizza in town." He thrust the slice back towards Gordy, who then knocked it from his hand.

The pizza hit the concrete with a smack. The other homeless suddenly froze and looked at it, smashed against the ground like roadkill, sauce splattered around it and the cheese oozing off the crust. The Pizza-pie Man's smile then morphed into a scowl. The whole world beneath the overpass fell silent and the air became thick with an angry intensity. For a moment, Gordy feared the man would throttle him and rip out his throat. He might have been lanky, but there was an air of menace around him and Gordy did not want to test him.

But, the smile returned. Slowly, it spread across his face and became a sinister grin. He began to chuckle—a low growl ricocheting through his throat. It rose into a hearty laugh before turning to an evil, squealing cackle. The vagrants around him began to turn pale and grab their stomachs. Their legs became wobbly and their heads started to hang. In seconds, they were retching, ready to vomit. Gordy backpedaled, sensing doom.

The Pizza-pie Man stopped laughing and frowned at Gordy, his mouth becoming a thin, sloping slit at the bottom of his face. He threw down the pizza box with force, leaned his head back, and let loose the most haunting howl Gordy ever heard. It sounded like multiple bloodthirsty wolves screeching in unison. It got louder and became so intense that Gordy imagined the man's head morphing into a train whistle. He expected smoke to begin rolling from the asshole's face. But what happened instead was far worse—far more horrifying—and even more fantastic.

The six hobos started throwing up large red chunks and thick white substances Gordy could not identify. They gagged and hacked, barfing up some sick liquid. It splattered on the ground like tomato soup. The other substance dangled from their mouths like thick curtains, swinging back and forth, as if caught in the breeze, before dripping to the ground. They all then started to quiver and scream. Slowly, their skin began to steam and crack, their blood, now clotted, busted through to the surface. The Pizza-pie Man kept howling, but no longer in a constant, flat sound, but in a rhythm, in a code, like a language or incantation. The homeless screamed harder as their skin started sliding from their bones—bones that began to crack and break, making nerve-shattering snapping sounds that made Gordy cringed in horror as he watched the vagrants collapse, as if they were being demolished from the inside. They dropped to the ground in flat, circular heaps, their skin spreading along their broken bones. Their blood pooled in between, and their innards pushed up through the melted dermis.

Once the street trash had finished melting, Gordy smelled the mixture of blood and cheese heavy in the air. The Pizza-pie Man stopped howling and looked around at the six round human puddles near him. To Gordy they looked like large pizzas: the crunched-up bones comprised the crust, and the melted skin was the cheese. Viscera were the toppings and the blood became the sauce. Now he understood why the stranger was so generous, and he was glad he declined the dinner invitation.

Without a word, the Pizza-pie Man pointed and the undulating mounds of bubbling cheese began to rotate and move towards Gordy. The human pizzas made sick squishy sounds as they twirled forward. Gordy kept backing up, moving beneath the shadow of the overpass, until his back hit the wall. He watched in horror as the creatures converged on him. The bony crust scratched and scraped along the concrete, white flecks breaking away as they moved. Where the bone fell away, the cheese would stick to the street, only to disconnect with a loud suction.

Gordy moved sideways along the wall as the pizzas closed in. The sinister Pizza-pie Man walked behind them, grinning and pointing in his direction. The discarded crust cracked beneath his feet. Long streaks of grease and blood trailed behind the trembling mounds. They drew ever nearer, and as they got closer each one's cheese began to rise from the crumbling plates of bone beneath them. Just before they swallowed Gordy, he woke from his horror and ran the length of the overpass, dashing across the lot towards some basketball courts.

"Faster!" he heard the Pizza-pie Man yell. "Catch him!"

Gordy fled across the concrete and the street cheese followed. Almost all of the bone had dissipated from the pies, ground into dust along the street.

They were now just piles of human cheese oozing along in pursuit of him. He could hear them slithering along the road, not far behind. The closest was only a few feet away and gaining.

"Leave me alone!" he screamed.

The fifteen-foot high fence around the basketball court was not far. Several men were embroiled in a couple of fast-paced games across two sets of goals and didn't even notice the homeless man running their way. When he burst through the gate, slamming it against the chain link fence and rattling the entire structure, the games ceased. Gordy quickly shut the gate and backed away.

"What the hell are you doing?" asked one man amidst a lot of grumbling.

Gordy backed into the middle of the court, speechless and pointing. All the players, who had first looked upon him with confusion and consternation, now followed the path his finger indicated. When they looked out beyond the fence, they started mumbling swears and questions at the sight of the odd blobby masses rolling towards them.

"Man, what's that shit?" asked one.

"I don't know," replied another.

Many inquiries were uttered, but none felt the fear that Gordy did, for their eyes had not seen what his had seen. He backed up to the far end of the courts as the giant mounds of melted skin and cheese began to force their way inside. The fence would not keep them back; they were oozing in between the mesh, forcing their gelatinous forms through the holes in the link. The bottom of the fence pushed forward and the tops rattled as the blobs entered.

Gordy started climbing the fence. "Run!" he called out. "Get out!"

None of the men listened; they just stared in awe. A couple of them walked over to the cheese to inspect it, but found only doom awaiting them.

One pile wrapped a thick arm around a man's ankle and pulled him into its mass. The contact seared his skin and he began to scream. As he was pulled slowly into the cheese, like Quint into the mouth of Jaws, his body began to melt. The heat from the thing was scorching, and the flesh sizzled and smoked at the slightest touch. His body soon melted and became part of the cheese collective.

The men began hollering, desperate to get away. Those who had first approached the pizzas were also consumed. Another man was attacked by a mound of cheese raising itself high off the ground and falling upon him like a tidal wave. When it fell over his body, it pulled his skin off immediately, leaving only his skeleton standing, which burst through the cheese as it slid down his form. But his frame did not last long. The burn was so intense that the bone dissolved and melded with the flabby creature.

Gordy made it to the top of the cage. The other men were slow to react and stood no chance. They were slaughtered like animals. Below him, Gordy heard the sizzles and pops of their bodies being reduced to jelly. Their bodies bubbled and burned as they were eaten alive by the rolling cheese beasts. Gordy descended about halfway on the other side before jumping down. He hit the ground, lost his balance, and fell on his ass. Before leaping up, he looked at the carnage before him. The entire layout of the courts was a sea of cheese as the men who had been playing were completely swallowed, with nothing left behind to remember them by— except the cheese they had now become.

From the opposite side, Gordy heard the evil laughter of the Pizza-pie Man. He looked across and saw him standing against the fence, his fingers locked around the mesh. He made eye contact and kept laughing as he too forced his way through the fence, turning into an oozy substance and reforming, then stepped onto the court. He walked across the cheese without sinking, making his way to the corner of the cage diagonal from where Gordy sat. The Pizza-pie Man then walked right up the fence, without using his hands, and stood atop the cage, looking down at him.

"Where do you think you will go, you worthless derelict? Do you think anyone will care for your dilemma? You are nothing. Nothing! And you will soon be consumed, as will everyone else!" He held up his hands and started cackling at the Heavens.

Gordy jumped up and fled in terror without looking back. Survival was his paramount motivation, but he also had to warn people of this impending chaos. He just hoped they would listen.

Try as he did, Gordy's warnings went unheeded. People treated him as just another raving homeless lunatic. Most just derided him, hollered oaths at him, and a few even shoved him away by his scraggily, dirty face. He tried to tell them but they didn't listen. He never considered that proclaiming, "The cheese is killing people", might make him sound insane.

The cheesy void rolled right through the town, claiming victims everywhere it went; and for every victim swallowed, a new mound of cheese formed. Soon, the initial six had multiplied into an army of a dozen or more. That army then multiplied, covering the streets and incinerating everything it touched. The cycle continued until it seemed the monsters covered the streets.

A jogger running along a quiet path through a small wooded area didn't think anything of the sudden overwhelming aroma of pizza that wafted to her from beyond the trees. With her earphones in, she didn't hear the heavy crunching of leaves or the squawks and cries of the birds and squirrels it enveloped as it flowed along the ground to her left. She also didn't hear the slapping and sucking of a second slab slithering up behind her. When the first pile left the woods and rolled onto her path, she stopped suddenly and yanked out her earphones.

"What the hell?" she said as the cheese churned her way.

When she turned to run, she stepped right into the putrefied prowler behind her. Her shoe melted almost immediately, welding itself to her skin. She screamed as the cheese rolled over her feet and up her legs. Blood gushed from the curling skin, burning off from the knees down before the heat cauterized the wounds. She tried to break away but couldn't. The other pile of cheese rolled up behind her and leapt into the air, wrapping around her upper body. It burned so hot and fast that as the cheese passed through the air, it was able to rip her torso from the lower half of her body, leaving the other pile to swallow her legs. Her upper-half was practically nonexistent by the time the cheese hit the ground.

A man driving down an empty stretch of highway found himself surrounded by several boiling pools of cheese. Zigzagging around the street, he had managed to dodge a few. But, he soon ran out of space. They had converged upon him. His Volvo screeched as he slammed on the brakes. The man peered ahead, seeing the road was covered in this cheesy substance. The collective gathered along the road, ominously circling him. Steam as thick as mist on a warm, rainy morning floated up from them, smoking up the street and unleashing the stink of red sauce and blood.

"What the hell is going on?" he asked himself.

The ring of cheese grew tighter, so he gunned the car for a getaway. As he raced towards the monster ahead, he'd hoped it would move. But it didn't. His tires hit the blob and were instantly stuck. He pressed the gas harder; the tire spun, throwing little cheese chunks through the air, but the car remained stuck, bucking and floating like a truck gone mudding. Soon, his tires exploded from the heat, the smell of burned rubber mixing with dairy and rot.

The car dropped deeper into the mound, melting away the metal. The steam found its way inside and burned his face at three-hundred degrees. The door beside him dissolved and the windows shattered. The cheese poured in and began to burn away his clothes, then his skin, before turning his bones into a liquid that would soon become another hungry killer.

Three young siblings pedaled their bikes with all their might, fleeing from the cheese that pursued them. Danny, the youngest and smallest of them, who had just turned thirteen, was lagging behind. Toni, his sister and the middle-child of fifteen, was trying to hang back enough to stay with Danny, despite the immense fear that was tingling through her body. Red, about to turn seventeen, pedaled far ahead of them both, not because he didn't give a shit about them, but because he wanted to find a secure spot where they all could hide from the ever-gaining strange thing that was following them. He knew they could not outrun it and finding a high ground was their only chance.

They had been biking along a path through the park when they saw the cheese roll over a bridge that crossed a ditch by the entrance. As it crossed, they saw parts of the mass drip between the cracks. By the time it reached the other side, the wood had melted and the bridge crumbled. There was a group of friends in its way and they didn't notice the tub of lard creeping up behind them. When the sound of the falling bridge caused them to turn around, the cheese took them. Soon, they were all thrashing about beneath its burning blanket. They died screaming before they too became mindless pools.

That's when the kids started pumping their legs as hard as they could. But, they could not escape the cheese so easily. It felt their tires vibrating along the ground, and its greasy, squishy form began to hunt. They thought they had enough of a head start, but were quickly losing ground. Soon, Red saw that their only hope was an average-sized tree with a few thick branches near the edge of the road.

"To the tree," he pointed.

When he reached it, he skidded to a halt, threw down his bike, and started climbing. It took Danny and Toni a few seconds to catch up. The cheese was about twenty feet behind. Danny was too short to reach the lowest branch and began to frantically scramble up the tree.

Red reached out. "Take my hand, Danny. Lift him up, Toni!"

Toni was a strong girl. She grabbed Danny's waist and said, "Put your feet on the trunk and push, then reach."

Danny did as told, and his fingers were almost brushing Red's. But, the cheese was closing in. Red screamed for Danny to reach harder, and he did. Toni pushed up with all her strength and her two brothers locked hands, but Danny almost pulled Red right off his branch.

"Come on, Danny!" Red yelled. "Climb!"

"Hurry up!" Toni cried as she waited for Danny to get in the tree so she could climb to safety.

But there was no time. The filthy cheese was only a few feet away. It had sucked up all of the grime along the ground to go along with the carcasses and it smelled of dirt and death. Toni sought a smaller branch to her left, pressed a foot on the tree and leapt for it, extending her left arm as high as it would go. She managed to grab the branch and dangle just a few feet above the sludgy predator.

As the river of cheese rolled by, a large portion leapt up, grabbing for her like a giant oozy arm, and snatched her by the waist. The immense heat instantly claimed her lower half, ripping through it like butter. Her upper body managed to hang on for a few seconds, but she was already dead, and her fingers slipped from the branch, sending the rest of her into the cheese.

Red pulled Danny harder as the cheese rose up, like a soufflé from Tophet. He managed to pull his little brother to relative safety, but the cheese kept coming. Red quickly broke a thick branch from the tree and climbed onto another branch to his right. It was a little lower, so he had a better angle to stab at the rising mound of mozzarella. He turned the sharp wood like a spear and began poking at it, stabbing heated holes into the flab. Steam burst forth from the wounds and seared his skin. He dropped the branch and cried out as his eyes turned to jelly in their sockets. He was unconscious when the soft, burning arms extended upwards and yanked him down to his death.

And the cheese rose on, reaching up onto branches, melting the wood. Danny climbed and climbed, all the way to the top. But the weight of the mass and the heat from its burn splintered the wood beneath it, and Danny stood no chance of survival as he plummeted into the greasy heap.

James was taking a shit and didn't even know of the horrors outside. He was reading over some submissions he had received for his fledgling publishing company when, suddenly, the toilet began to rattle.

"What the bloody hell?" he said.

He had let some bowl-ringers before, but nothing like this. He felt the vibration beneath his feet. His ass started to get very hot. The water sloshed around in the bowl, and just as he was about to drop another doozy, all that water was absorbed by the thick substance bursting through the pipes.

The cheese went straight up his ass and coiled through his insides. The heat began to melt his internal organs instantly. He seized up as the burn wound its way through him. Soon, it was bursting through all his facial orifices. James was absorbed from the inside out and sucked down into the cheese.

Like a monster, it grew, winding its way through James's house, burning all walls and floors, peeling paint and drywall like a raging inferno. The entire house was reduced to a few planks of wood and some random shingles in its wake. It looked like an F4 tornado had taken it. Once its rampage was complete, the gooey mountain bounced away.

The town was in terror as the powerhouse pizzas rolled through, devouring all that lay in their paths. Gordy still tried to warn the people and they still wouldn't listen, not until they were running for their lives, literally trying to save their own skin. He did all he could. Now, he just wanted to survive. He found the tallest building in the city—some bank headquarters downtown—and ran up the stairs, shoving aside anyone that got in his path.

The building was not tall, only ten floors, but it would do. When he reached the top, he burst through the doorway and scrambled to the edge of the roof to survey the city. He smelled the cheese and burning flesh on the air. Screams from below assaulted his ears. He looked out and saw dozens upon dozens—perhaps even hundreds—of titanic pizzas tearing through town. A large assemblage had gathered at the base of his building, working its way up the sides.

Now even more frantic, he looked for a way out, but there was none. All the cheese balls were climbing, sticking to the wall like sludge, pushing their way up like slugs. He started to panic; he was going to die and turn into a large cheese pizza.

Then he heard laughter behind him. He turned and saw the hideous face of the Pizza-pie Man rising over the ledge on the far side. He held that pizza box in his hand, and his grin was as unapologetically sinister as before.

He approached Gordy, pulled open the box, and said, "Are you sure you don't want a piece now, Gordy?"

"Go away!" Gordy yelled and ran back to the door.

When he grabbed the knob, his hand sizzled and the Pizza-pie Man laughed.

"The cheese is always there, Gordy—waiting for you to enter, and waiting to enter you! If you choose to eat this slice, then you will become the predator, instead of being only a tiny bit of flavoring for its untamable appetite."

The Pizza-pie Man stood behind him now, so close Gordy could feel his presence. He turned and looked right into the man's hideous smile. The last slice was held before him, inches from his face.

"Eat it, Gordy. It's for the best."

Gordy balked. The Pizza-pie Man thrust the sizzling slice at him.

"Eat it or be eaten by it!" he warned.

Gordy looked around. On all sides, the cheese had reached the top and begun to climb over the ledges. He was out of time. He had to make his final move.

"Eat it or be eaten by it, huh?" he asked.

The Pizza-pie Man grinned. "Yes."

"Can you do both?"

The Pizza-pie Man's evil expression became confused—then alarmed when Gordy grabbed his wrist with his left hand and then pushed on his elbow with his right, bending the Pizza-pie Man's arm. Gordy wrestled the man's hand towards his creepy mouth; when it was almost there, Gordy kneed him in the balls, hoping the ominous freak possessed a pair.

Apparently, he did. The shot landed and the Pizza-pie Man groaned. Gordy shoved the last slice into his gaping mouth and forced it down his throat. He let go and punched the Pizza-pie Man in the stomach, causing him to gulp hard. The pizza slid further down his gullet and he began to gag and hold his throat. Gordy grabbed him by the collar and pushed him towards the ledge behind him. He found one spot not covered in cheese and pushed him over, sending him screaming to the ground.

Gordy leaned on the ledge and watched the Pizza-pie Man land in a giant ocean of cheese. There was no walking across it this time. When his eyes rolled back, his body sank into its yellow depths.

Once the Pizza-pie Man was gone, all the cheese stopped moving. That which was climbing began to drip slowly down the walls, receding across the rooftop, before sliding out of sight and falling to the streets below.

All across the city, the cheese ceased its onslaught and began to lose its burn. Though the dead were gone and the damage done, the advancement of the monstrous pizzas had halted. In less than an hour, all of them had gone cold, their cheese congealed and their toppings stale.

Gordy looked below him and saw cheese piled almost halfway up the building. He went to each side and saw the same sight. The entire building was surrounded by cold, hard cheese.

He left the roof and tried to take the stairs, but stopped on the seventh floor when he saw his path was blocked two floors down. The creatures had broken out all the windows and flooded the interior. The thick, coagulated mess now clogged the stairway and elevators like the arteries of a bad heart.

Gordy sat on the steps and started to laugh. His stomach rumbled and he wondered how long he would be stuck here.

MONSTERS OF WOODED HOLLOW

Despite his mother's wishes, Young William went wandering into the eerie Wooded Hollow one autumn evening before Halloween. She had always warned him that strange and peculiar people lurked there. But that didn't scare William. Nothing did—not ghosts, not nightmares, and not things that went bump in the night. Ever the fearless explorer, William crept out the backdoor at the onset of twilight, while his mother was preparing dinner and his father was lighting the fireplace in the sitting room, and ventured off into this infamous small valley at the edge of the neighborhood.

His mother wasn't the only one that showed concern regarding Wooded Hollow. His father also told him to stay away from there and scolded him if he mentioned the place. Many of his friends confessed that *their* parents warned them away from the desolate, shallow valley always covered in a dense, white fog, too.

"My mama says that the Devil lives there," his friend Timmy once said.

"My papa told me that his company used to cut wood from there, but stopped on account of monsters that walk through the fog," Timmy's cousin Donnie put in.

"No way," William responded. "I don't believe that. There's no such thing as monsters. And why would the Devil live there? Ain't he busy running Hell and bothering God?"

Timmy and Donnie both shook their heads.

"The Devil *is* there," Timmy insisted. "That's why fires are always burning there at night."

William stopped to consider this. He did recall seeing fires there before.

"And I hear monsters screaming out that way, too," Donnie said.

William also recalled hearing wails and howls echoing from the darkness near Wooded Hollow. He figured that they came from wild animals and he didn't buy into this silly nonsense about monsters and devils. So, he decided to prove it to his overly imaginative friends.

"I bet you there's nothing but animals in that hollow. And the fires are probably just hunters. There ain't no monsters. I'll prove it. I'll go out there at night and look around. You guys can come, too. How about it?"

Timmy and Donnie's eyes widened. They looked at each other, then back at William. When William met them with a challenging glare, they both shook their heads.

"No way," Timmy said. "I wouldn't go in there for a whole year's allowance."

"Yeah," Donnie said. "Me neither. And you shouldn't go in there either, William, or the Devil will eat you."

"If I see the Devil, I'll run," William declared.

"It won't matter! If you run from him, the monsters will hunt you down. Those are the Devil's monsters and they do what he says," Donnie said.

William chuckled. "Now I know you're just making that up. I'll go in there tomorrow night and tell you all if I see the Devil or not."

Now here he was, walking quickly across the damp grass of his large backyard, headed straight for Wooded Hollow. Evening zipped by and night fell fast; the moon was full and bright, and it lit a small, sparkling path along the wet blades of grass. William marched briskly, constantly looking back, more afraid that his parents would see him than he was of any monsters.

As he drew nearer, he detected the aroma of burning wood riding the soft breeze. Squinting to see better, he thought he might be able to discern a faint orange flicker lightly penetrating the heavy fog.

He stopped for a second to contemplate his decision to visit the hollow. He still didn't believe in monsters, but he did believe in humans – bad ones. One of his uncles was bad. He killed another man and took his money a few years ago. Ever since he'd heard about that, he had often feared that his uncle would come kill him, too. What if someone like his uncle was hiding in those woods?

Well, if he were, dummy, he wouldn't have a fire burning. That would give away his hiding spot, he told himself.

Determining that was sound logic, he ventured on, following the moonbeams sliding along the grass. In a few more minutes, he was on the short dirt road that led into the hollow. On each side of the path, rabbits leaped and possums meandered. Birds squeaked and flew away as William approached. When he was more than halfway down the path, a hellish howl resounded through the night, freezing him in place.

"That wasn't any animal I've ever heard," he said to himself. "That sounded human."

When the shriek rose up again, William lost his nerve and turned to go home. But a tall black shape standing on the path ahead made him stop.

"Where you think you're going, boy?" said a muffled male voice.

"I'm…uh…just going home," William stammered.

The man began walking towards him. As he crossed into the path of the moonlight, William could see he wore a disheveled black mask with flaccid horns sticking out of both sides. He carried a bundle of sticks in his right hand.

"Can't go home yet. You're just in time for the celebration."

Not caring to find out what the man meant, William turned back and ran towards the hollow. As he got closer, the fire became more evident. The fog grew thicker. Other sounds began to travel through the air, laughter that reminded him of cackling witches and roars that could only come from hellish beasts. He didn't care. He could not yet see them, so he did not know for sure what they were, but he had seen the frightening man behind him, and that man reminded him of his uncle.

Wooded Hollow was only a few yards away, the noises and smells growing more intense. Leaping shadows of what looked like flailing humans were dancing reflections in the firelight. Just before he reached the hollow, he looked back to see how close the man was to catching him. He was not there. William had somehow lost him, so he turned back towards the hollow just as he entered the thick mist around it.

Once inside the foggy hollow, William skidded to a halt and gasped in horror. He found the fire, and over it hung a bloody body, gutted and partially charred, its insides dangling from holes in its stomach. The skin on the legs and arms were cracked and black. Around it danced people in strange masks that resembled frightening creatures, some with long, pointy teeth, and others with devilish horns atop their heads. The dancing ceased, as did the howls and laughter. The masked dancers stood upright and began to crowd around him. Grinning green and red faces smeared with blood peered down at William.

The only face the young man could see in those masks was that of his uncle's. He didn't see the Devil, he didn't see monsters–those were not real–but bad humans like his uncle were, and now he was alone in the secluded hollow with them.

"Please," he said. "I won't tell anyone. Just let me go home."

"There is no home anymore. Not for you," said the muffled voice he'd heard before.

William turned around to see the man who had blocked his path earlier now standing behind him.

"You belong to the Hollow, now."

"Please," William begged.

Suddenly, the monstrous roar he heard previously rumbled through the night, rattling the hollow. It seemed to shake the trees and stir the fire. The people gathered around him now moved away. As they did, they unblocked William's view of the shadows just beyond the flames. A dark image began to move towards them. It brought with it an icy air. A terrifying wind that turned hearts to stone and set bones to quivering swirled around the approaching shadow.

When it stepped into the light of the fire, a terror beyond William's reckoning stood before him – the terror that Timmy and Donnie had been right about. Staring at him from the edge of darkness was the Devil–tall like the trees and red like the evening sunset, eyes as yellow as the moon; massive, spear-like horns, blacker than night, protruded from his forehead, dripping gore from their tips. Flanking him were giant, black, red-eyed canines baring their teeth, backs arched, bodies poised to attack.

The Devil pointed a smoldering finger, tipped with a dagger-like talon, at William and said in a voice made of granite and flame, "You have trespassed in my Hollow. Your home will now be with me."

The masked dancers laughed in unison and William passed out.

When he came to later, he found himself lying on his bed. The dread that had seized him began to ebb as he realized he was home. He sat up and rubbed his eyes.

"That was the worse dream I ever had."

"William," his mother called from the kitchen. "Dinner's ready."

William rose from bed and stretched, still trying to shake that horrifying dream. He opened his door and walked into the kitchen. The table was set but his mother was not in there.

"Mother?"

From the sitting room, she called, "Yes dear. I'll be there in just a minute."

William sighed and stood by the table, waiting on his parents. He was so hungry, he wanted to sit down and start eating, but had been taught it was rude to begin without the entire family gathered for the feast.

"Where's father?" he called to his mother.

She did not answer, so he asked again.

"Mother? Where's father?"

"I'm here, son."

The sound of his father's voice behind him gave William pause. Something about it was not normal. He stood up straight and did not turn, but spoke instead.

"Father? Is that you?"

"Yes, William, it is me. Turn around."

William began to shiver. He knew what was not right about his father's voice. It was muffled, just like the voice of the man in his dreams.

"I said turn around, son."

Slowly, William turned, and cried out when he saw his parents standing in the kitchen doorway. His father, wearing the mask of the man he had seen in what he thought had been a dream, stood there, holding the large bundle of sticks. His mother was beside his father, wearing a bloody green mask with horns and a long, serpentine tongue jutting out between two vicious-looking teeth.

"Mother? Father?" William whined.

"Yes dear," his mother said. "We know where you were."

"We told you not to go to Wooded Hollow," his father said. "But you disobeyed, and *He* saw you."

William began to cry. "I believe in the Devil now! And the monsters! But I won't tell anyone. I swear!"

"It is too late son. There's nothing we can do," said his father.

"What are you going to do to me?" William asked.

"Sit and eat, dear," his mother told him. "You must eat. You must be fat for the Lord of the Hollow, for the feast is about to start.

UNDEAD FROM OUTER SPACE

I scraped the guts of the giant zombie off my boots after I barricaded the door behind me. I'd been trapped in the house for several days and was sure that I was the last person alive in town. Provisions ran low and I had to chance a trip to the nearest market, which was about a mile away. I didn't see any other living people during the trip, just some eviscerated carcasses and those rancid, rotting corpses that practically fell from the sky.

Yes—fell from the sky. Not literally, they didn't drop from the Heavens like rain. They arrived in flying saucers, but I don't think they were the ones flying them. The crafts' sparkling lights could be seen all over town as they floated through the sky—large, round ships, as fast and bright as falling stars. They dropped to the ground and opened their hatches, then out came the creeps. It didn't take long for them to get to work, either. Everyone that was near to them became ripped and torn morsels for the flesh-craving visitors.

After dropping off a few dozen ghouls each, the ships ascended and quickly sped away, vanishing into the night. These weren't like zombies from the movies, either. These creatures had decent motor skills; they could run and talk and I even saw them use pitchforks, bats, and other various objects to kill the townsfolk. We were outnumbered, so I ran like hell back to my farmhouse on the edge of town and barricaded myself in.

The home had been in our family since before this town was established nearly two hundred years ago. My aunt and brother lived here with me and I had no idea where they were. We don't mess with cell phones and the landline was out, so I couldn't make any calls. They were both at work when this all happened. I was just coming home, walking along the darkened road from the mill to the house, when the invasion began. Not many people live near us, so that might be why I didn't see anybody else when I went to the market. But after seeing what these zombies could do, I didn't have much hope for anyone else that might have been caught outside; and, if there were any other survivors, it's probable they were holed up in their homes like me, waiting out the riot.

The zombies could be dropped with a shot to the brain, like any zombies on TV. But they were harder to hit. They were capable of hiding and strategizing. They snuck up on people and hid in dark places, such as patches of woods, or behind bales of hay. I saw a couple break Granny Johnson's window out with a chair leg and storm her house. So, I knew I had to reinforce our home good to keep them out.

I help build and renovate houses as a side job, so it didn't take much for me to hammer up some boards. The material was readily available. Everything I needed—wood, nails, hammer, drill—were in the shed out back. Was it dangerous for me to go out there? Not at all. A few years back, I'd erected a twelve-foot high privacy fence out of some of the hardest wood I could get my hands on and reinforced it with leaning beams plunged two feet into the ground. No one was getting in back here—not even undead creatures as astute as these were.

But, let me tell you that before I could completely board up the house, I had to do some fighting. I'm no small guy—a hair over six foot and about two-hundred-and-thirty pounds, some muscle and some fat—but I'm not a hulking man, either. But, I know how to scrap. A couple of the bastards that broke in found that out. Now, believe you me, some of them can throw down, too. But, not like me. I punched and kicked my way right through them, tossing them through the empty windows and out the back door, smashing in heads with whatever random objects lay about the house: a pipe, a wrench, a frying pan, and even a lamp—it all made good weaponry for me to ward off these undead invaders.

One thing I noticed when I was fighting the putrid intruders is that they were most definitely human—or, were at one time. Unless they came from somewhere where the inhabitants look just like us, these were long-dead people straight from planet Earth. Why in the hell they came here in spaceships, I don't know.

Some of them were pretty vocal. I could hear a few in the yard just beyond my porch yelling for me to come out. Telling me they would come in and get me sooner or later, and if I surrendered they'd make my death quick—a mighty weak bargain, if you ask me. I went to the door and yelled through the crack.

"Dead is dead—quick or slow, what's it matter? If you want me, come on in and get me," is what I said.

"We *are* death," several replied in unison.

Though that haunting declaration gave me some awful chills, I wasn't going to show that to them. "Well then, I ain't buying. Now go on back to wherever you came from or you'll get blown to bits. I got me a gun in here and I *will* start shooting."

"There's nothing you can do, nothing *any* of you can do. We are endless. We are *eternal.*"

"Not if I put a bullet between your eyes. I've seen y'all drop."

"But we will return. *They* will bring us back. *They* will always bring us back."

I didn't quite know what the hell they were talking about, or whom *"they"* were, but I assumed it had to do with the spaceships. Done with that conversation, I went about my business adding extra wood to the windows I had already boarded up.

The house was a veritable fortress by the time I was done. Heavy wood lay in layers against the doors and windows, all strapped in by steel bars that I had drilled into the walls. The only way out lay through the front door, which I had reinforced with several metal slide-bars to keep the dead from coming in—which it was unlikely they would at this point, anyway. The porch outside was closed off by a brick wall, and after taking a few ghouls out with some weird Scottish sword my pa had given me years ago—said it represented our ancestral clan, or some crazy shit like that—I went about securing it, too. When I added the porch sometime back, I put up the thick walls without windows because I didn't want any prowlers peeking in. Our little town wasn't high in crime, but it was damn country, so there was always a chance of some depraved lunatic lurking about the property. We had never had any incidents involving trespassers since then, so the porch had seemed like a wasted effort. That perception was sure changing, now.

While I had built one hell of a protective wall—one that would sure make Donald Trump proud—throughout the house, it was a bitch getting in and out of it. Naturally, I couldn't close the bars when I left since they were on the other side of the door, so I had to rely on the stability of the porch to keep the space ghouls at bay in my absence. I snatched up the sword, opting to leave my rifle so I wouldn't attract more zombies with gunfire, and headed out to the market. There were only a few monsters in the yard when I left, and I ended them with ease. When I came back, there must have been near to a dozen, and they were spry. Like I said before—I'm a tough son of a bitch, but I ain't the Man of Steel. I can only tango with so many at once.

It was a hell of a battle. I spent a lot of goddamn time running around the front yard, kicking, punching, and swinging my sword like a madman before all the fuckers went down. I chopped off arms, legs, necks, and even skewered one through the side of the head, cheek to temple. The final zombie remaining, which was blocking the door, was a titanic brute that towered over me like a tree. He was slow, but his hands were the size of my head and I swear the creature was probably a professional wrestler in life. I couldn't get a decent stab in on his cranium, so I had to do what any good lumberjack would do (and I used to be a lumberjack!)—I started chopping at the trunk. I would have started with the branches, but with my luck, the fucker would have snatched the sword and I'd be forced to engage in fisticuffs with the monster, and I don't think I would have won that tussle.

Anyway, I stabbed and sliced and swiped until that big bastard's bubbly blood had literally rained o'er me. By the time the fight was over, I looked like Sissy Spacek after she'd just accepted her prom queen win in *Carrie,* only I wasn't wearing a gown and I didn't have telekinetic powers. All I had was my sword, and that did the trick. I cut a large gash through his guts, dropping him to his knees right in front of me. The innards splashed out, hitting the ground and spitting out body juice. Wearing bloodstained overalls was becoming a good look for me.

I had to wade through the ogre's guts to get to the porch, and I squished and slipped my way up the steps and into the house. Once back in, I did a thorough sweep to make sure I was alone—and I was.

Now, here's the thing: I sure hope these zombies differ from those in the movies in more ways than just possessing heightened motor skills. I also hope their bites don't turn you into no zombie, neither. Yes sir, you bet'cha—I went and got me nibbled on during that brawl. Nibbled is a nice way to put it. One of those suckers bit a good plug out of my forearm. It wasn't like a huge chunk of flesh was torn away, but the teeth went in deep and the blood sprayed out like a trick flower that squirts water. Thankfully, the gargantuan at the door isn't the one that bit me, or I'd probably had my arms snapped in two by his hippopotamus teeth.

I went right to washing the wound. I poured on all the disinfectants I could find: hydrogen peroxide, Neosporin, many squirts of antibacterial soap, and some good ole skin-searing water hot enough to steam up the bathroom and turn my skin red. I was glad to see that, once I was done, the wound did not hurt or give any indication of having an infection. It doesn't mean there wasn't one, but if it was something that was going to turn me into some body-eating deadhead like them shits outside, I figured it would probably be hurting something awful at this juncture.

After I cleaned and dressed my wound and started putting the non-perishable food away (good thing I love noodles and rice), I started going about the house double-checking all windows and doors, making sure no one could sneak in on me. Once I felt secure enough in that respect, I prepared me some noodles with a lot of pepper and butter (better use that while the electricity is still going) and decided to take a seat at the upstairs window—the only one I hadn't boarded up—to watch for my aunt and brother. If they came running, I was going to be right there to let them in.

The second floor is small, much less space than the first, and the ceiling is lower, coming to a point overhead. There's a room overlooking the front yard. I went to a small, round window and planted myself in a rickety old chair that probably came over to America with the first of my ancestors. As I gazed out, chomping down my twenty-eight cent dinner (which I got for a twenty-eight cent discount on account of the market being abandoned at the onset of the apocalypse), I saw someone coming through the field across from our property. There were no more zombies (and I mean literally no more; those I killed had inexplicably vanished) and no sign of men—just this lone figure marching across the grass. He was tall and lean, dressed in some strange silver and black attire, with a wide-brimmed fedora atop his head. He carried something long and dark in his hands and, though I couldn't see his face in any detail, I could tell by his rigid posture and determined gait that he was approaching with a purpose.

When he got to the edge of the yard, I could see his grayish face and large black eyes, favoring the popular consensus among abductees of what aliens look like. Other than that, he looked like a man. But he was tall—really tall—like, he probably could have stood on his tiptoes and looked right in the upstairs window with just a little hop.

His clothes resembled the garb of a Calvinist preacher from the 1800s, only the belt, shoes, and undershirt were silver; everything else was black. I could see he had some patches of rot on his face, and his hands looked partly decayed. In those hands, though, is where the real story lay: the man/creature was carrying some sort of shotgun and he looked damned determined to use it.

"I know you're in there," he called in a clear, high-pitched voice that echoed as if he'd yelled into a drainpipe.

I leaned forward and opened the window. "Well, good for you. I ain't hiding."

The stranger immediately aimed his rifle and fired at the window. The shot was good and the glass shattered. I hit the floor and started crawling out of the room. Another slug hit the wall behind me. Once I was out, I ran down the hall as another bullet flew through the walls. I pounded down the steps and went into the living room and grabbed my Mossberg 500, then turned and ran back upstairs to the broken window. When I looked out, he was nowhere in sight.

Hanging my gun partly out the window, swiveling it around, I searched the perimeter for my target.

"Where you at, you dirty bastard?" I whispered.

I couldn't figure out if he was a zombie, man, or alien—or somehow all three. It was a preposterous notion, but I'd seen so much crazy shit that day, my disbelief in many things had been suspended indefinitely. But, if he was a zombie, I was sure hoping to God that they all didn't know how to use guns.

A loud explosion downstairs stole my attention.

"There you are," I said and fled from the room.

I was back downstairs in the living room in just a few seconds, standing face to face with the long, lanky man whose hat brushed the ceiling. He had shattered the front door from its hinges, even busting up the sliding steel bars. That must have been one powerful gun, or he was He-Man Hercules.

"You broke my door, dickhead. Who are you?" I asked, aiming my Mossberg.

He lowered his weapon and held out a ridiculously large hand with fingers longer than butcher knives. The palm was pale, the skin flabby, and there were tears around the edges.

"I am Death."

"Yeah, it seems like you all say that."

"I am the New Beginning."

"Are you Death or the New Beginning? Make up your damned mind."

"We have come. We've waited years, but we have come. This world is ours."

The creature's voice was grating my nerves, running jagged nails across my eardrums. If insects could speak loud enough to communicate with us, they would likely sound like this asshole.

"You think so? I hope you brought a powder keg, pal. We ain't giving it up without a fight."

"There is no fight. You have already lost. Man will fall."

"Well, your victory won't start here in my house, freak."

I squeezed the trigger and blew the bastard's hand off. He might have been strong, but his hand was just a hand, and it exploded and littered the room in tiny, obliterated pieces.

He screamed and started to raise his gun, but I shot him right in the head, sending him sailing out onto the porch. His body landed on the steps and rolled out into the yard. He struggled off the ground for a second and stumbled a few feet before falling onto his back.

His fedora fluttered to the floor at the threshold. I picked it up and put it on (a perfect fit, surprisingly enough), then walked out into the yard and stood over him. He was dying; his head was parted from the nose up, and some strange jelly oozed out in black and green undulating globs. Though he should have been dead, his eyes blinked and I could hear him breathing.

"It's no use," he screeched.

Three more zombies were approaching, so I took aim and blew their heads off one-by-one. After they'd fallen, I aimed the barrel at the visitor.

"I got one left. You want to tell me why you're here?"

"I have already told you," his voice squelched.

"Did you bring all these undead bastards to our planet?"

"Not me, but my kind."

"Why?"

"The world will be ours. For years we have watched you, studied you. We have taken you. Now, we have brought you back, and you will take this world for us."

"Look, I don't really know what the hell you think you're gonna do, or how you plan to take over the world, but let me tell you something, chief, you brought all these zombies to this here town and for what? To have the lot of them blown apart by one man barricaded in his house? If I did what I did, what do you think the rest of humanity will be able to do?"

The invader then laughed, loudly, arrogantly, and said, "This is only the beginning—a test—the real invasion still comes."

"Is that right? Well, when they get here, you better believe Earth will be ready."

The laughter stopped and he said, "It is already here."

The creature raised the hand that was still intact, unfurled a long finger, and pointed to the sky behind me.

"Look," he said.

I turned, and in the sky, I saw a fleet of countless ships, hovering and moving against the evening. Many were descending far off in the distance, vanishing behind the tree lines and hilltops, and many more were coming from the dark reaches of space. If those things were carrying more zombie hordes, then the weird, dying stranger was right—we were in trouble.

The creature laughed as hard as he could until he coughed up some more black goo. He choked and sputtered for a moment before his head fell back and he died. I looked back to the sky and watched a ship land behind the house. The bridge lowered and down it ran an army of screaming zombies.

I turned back to the dead creature, and he was gone.

I scratched my head. "The fuck?"

Zombies were running amuck, going this way and that. I glanced at my house and its shattered front door.

"Shit," I said. "I don't have enough bullets for this fight."

The screaming mass rushed my way, so I turned and fled into the black shadows of the woods, with no intention of stopping to look back.

Thank you for reading! If you like the book, please leave a review on Amazon and Goodreads. Even if you don't like it, please still leave a review.

To keep up with more Nightmare Press news, join the Anubis Press Dynasty on Facebook.

Jacob Floyd is a horror and paranormal nonfiction author from Louisville, KY, where he lives with his wife Jenny, his three dogs (Tarzan, Pegasus, and Snow White – aka BooBoo), and three cats (Baloo, Narnia, and Pandora Opossum). He and Jenny are known as the Frightening Floyds and have written several books about haunted locations and legends. They are the owners of Anubis Press, Nightmare Press, and Wild West Press. They also own and operate two historic ghost walks in the Louisville area: *Jacob Floyd's Shepherdsville History and Haunts Tour* and *Jacob Floyd's NuLu History and Haunts Tour*. You can find both tour pages on Facebook.

Jacob is a long-time horror fan who grew up on 80s horror, R.L. Stine's *Goosebumps* series, and the old sci-fi and horror TV anthologies. He is a fan of authors Clive Barker, Richard Laymon, James Herbert, Robert McCammon, and Poppy Z. Brite, just to name a few.

NIGHT OF THE POSSUMS

JACOB FLOYD

The night of the possums began on a chilly autumn morning around 2am in late October.

On a dark country road, a young man is torn to shreds by wild animals. The news of his grisly death rocks the town. When a similar death occurs later that day, the town is in the grips of fear.

In rural Bardstown, Kentucky, opossums have risen up against the populace. People are being maimed and devoured throughout the city. These are not your ordinary opossums, either: they are smarter, stronger, faster, and far more vicious—some larger than any opossum anyone has ever seen, growing as long as four feet and as heavy as fifty pounds, with teeth capable of cleaving bone.

As the flesh-eating scourge quickly spreads from one end of Bardstown to the other, a few of those who survived the attacks band together in an attempt to eradicate the maniac marsupials. But, the number of the beasts grows by the hour and the force becomes too insurmountable; the survivors soon realize escape is their only option.

But, beyond the berserk behavior of the carnivorous creatures is a darker secret—something ancient and unnatural that threatens all those who are bitten. Before anyone can find out what is driving these opossums to kill, the survivors must battle their way through the merciless onslaught of claws and teeth and leave the threat of Bardstown behind them.

Thank you for reading! If you like the book, please leave a review on Amazon and Goodreads. Even if you don't like it, please still leave a review.

To keep up with more Nightmare Press news, join the Anubis Press Dynasty on Facebook.

www.ingramcontent.com/pod-product-compliance
Lightning Source LLC
Chambersburg PA
CBHW051922220626
47052CB00003B/554